Farewell,
Thunder Moon

Farewell, Thunder Moon

MAX BRAND™

A Great Western Adventure™

Sagebrush
Large Print Westerns

Library of Congress Cataloging in Publication Data

Brand, Max, 1892-1944.
    Farewell, Thunder Moon / Max Brand.
        p.   cm.   — (A great western adventure)
    ISBN 1-57490-123-0 (hardcover : alk. paper)
    1. Large type books. I. Title. II. Series.
[PS3511.A87F36   1998]
813'.52—dc21   98-15046
                                                            CIP

Cataloguing in Publication Data is available from
the British Library and the National Library of Australia.

Sagebrush Large Print Westerns are published in the United States
and Canada by Thomas T. Beeler, Publisher, Box 659, Hampton Falls,
New Hampshire 03844-0659. ISBN 1-57490-123-0

Published in the United Kingdom, Eire, and the Republic of South Africa
by Isis Publishing Ltd, 7 Centremead, Osney Mead, Oxford OX2 0ES
England. ISBN 0-7531-5882-5

Published in Australia and New Zealand by Australian Large Print Audio
& Video Pty Ltd, 17 Mohr Street, Tullamarine, Victoria, 3043, Australia.
ISBN 1-86340-752-9

Manufactured in the United States of America by BookCrafters, Inc.

ACKNOWLEDGMENTS

An earlier version of this work was published under the title "Thunder Moon Goes White" by George Owen Baxter in *Western Story Magazine* (11/3/28).

"Thunder Moon Goes White." Copyright © 1928 by Street & Smith Publications, Inc. Copyright © renewed 1956 by Dorothy Faust. Acknowledgment is made to Condé Nast Publications, Inc., for their cooperation.

The text of this book is taken from the original typescript by Frederick Faust.

The name Max Brand™ and Great Western Adventure by Max Brand™ are registered trademarks with the U. S. Patent Office and cannot be used for any purpose without express written permission.

Farewell, Thunder Moon

CHAPTER ONE

THE PAWNEES ARE OUT

OUT OF THE HILLS CAME A RED RIDER. HE WENT LIKE the wind, his long, heavy hair streaming across his shoulders. He was a big man. All the Cheyennes were big.

The pony beneath him seemed absurdly inadequate to carry such a bulk, and yet it continued to run. It was polished with sweat which ran down the to the middle of its belly and, at the parting of the hair, dripped off in a steady shower. Where the stirrup leathers or the knees of the rider touched, the horse was rubbed to lather. Lather formed, too, behind the elbows of the running pony and before the stifle. Foam from its gaping mouth blew back and flecked its shoulders, its breast. Its ears were flattened with labor and with agony for the Cheyenne in the saddle punished it forward with the most determined cruelty. He worked over the struggling animal, appearing to pay little attention to the direction in which it ran, but exerting all his ingenuity to torment additional speed out of it.

It was far spent. It went down a slope with a vain effort to lengthen its stride sufficiently. It struck the following rise with a drunken stagger, and the Cheyenne snarled brutally at it, and struck it with his club.

Torment or not, it was going only at a hard gallop when the Indian topped the rise and saw before him another warrior in the hollow beneath, a man who had heard that violent approach, the hoofs of the tired pony beating and scattering the rocks. He of the hollow had

1

halted his horse—a lofty and noble-appearing chestnut —and had swung into the crook of his left arm a long-barreled rifle. At wait, he regarded the other.

From a distance seeing the rider of the chestnut, the speeding warrior began to make frantic signs, and drove straight down on the other. As he came by, still he kept his animal at a gallop. The big chestnut was turned then and galloped easily at his side.

"You are one of Thunder Moon's men!" exclaimed the rider of the pony. "I tell you by your horse and by your rifle. Tarawa has put you here to relay the warning to our people. Ride on! Do not spare the tall horse this day. Use whip and club on him. Make him fly, because fly he must. The Pawnees are out! Spotted Bull is leading them. I myself have lain for two hours and watched them, and counted them. They are a host. They are well armed. Their horses are good. They travel slowly, like men wishing to keep their horses and themselves fresh for a battle. Even now perhaps they have picked up my trail and are rushing behind me like wolves, but now you carry on the warning."

The second warrior said not a word in reply. He took his rifle and handed it to the other, who carried a war bow alone. He gave him also a pouch of ammunition, so that if the brave were indeed overtaken by the flying Pawnees, he might give a good account of himself until help arrived from the Cheyenne camp.

After that, he sent the chestnut flying. No Indian pony could have matched the speed of that Thoroughbred. It devoured the ground with mighty bounds, and the rider urged it neither with hand nor heel. Only with his voice he talked to it, and the big horse smoked on over the ground like a red mist caught on a storm wind. It was not for lack of will that the rider failed to strike the

2

mare, for again and again his hand rose and hung suspended, as one who well knew that if there were a mark or blemish upon the beautiful coat of the mare, he would be called to a strict accounting when he entered the camp.

Presently he broke out of the hills into a stretch of gently rolling ground. A river angled sharply out of the highlands, and then rolled smoothly away along the undulations of this fatherland of the prairies which, further eastward, drew off as level as a gigantic playing field. Where the river swung in a wide bend through this pleasant country—treeless, but spotted with drifting lines of shrubs here and there and rich with tall grass that swished about the legs of the running chestnut— there was an Indian village placed at a suitable distance from the water's edge. One could tell that the tribe prospered by the whiteness of the teepees and by the numbers of horses which moved in herds nearby, under the care of many keen-eyed boys. A thin stream of people went from the village to the water and back— women to wash, or girls to carry in water or wood, or boys to frolic and play and make themselves strong. Oh, glorious youth of the red man, too proud to labor!

The warrior on the red mare, taking note of all of this, smiled a little in pride, and rode on at a greater pace than ever, for the mare was keen at the sight of her home. Like a flung lance, horse and man darted into the circles of the teepees and, in the innermost circle, flung himself to the ground. The mare, sliding to a halt on braced legs pony fashion, cast up a billow of dust before her, for here the grass had long been worn away and the surface of the ground had not been scoured recently by a heavy wind.

There were three teepees close together in this

3

innermost circle and into the nearest of them—a noble, gaudily painted lodge—the warrior turned. He first struck against the board which was posted near the entrance. A voice spoke within. He lifted the flap and entered.

Inside, squatted at the back of the lodge upon a folded buffalo robe, was a chief who wore a hideous mask of a face. In close fight with the enemy he had lost one eye, his right cheek had been slashed across three separate times, and the flesh had gathered above the ghastly pallid furrows of the wounds. A side stroke with a battle axe, glancing off the top of his head, had laid one whole side of it bare and, though around this bare spot the hair grew luxuriously, still at the best it was only a partial scalp which he would offer the hand of a victorious enemy. Nevertheless, to his people he was a handsome object. His wounds were proofs of his dauntless valor, and he was in fact the war chief of this detachment of the great Cheyenne nation. He was now smoking a long pipe whose bowl was of the true pipe rock, and he rose and greeted the other with a resounding: "How!"

"You have brought news, Young Snake," he said. "Will you eat first and then smoke, or first will you speak?"

"The Pawnee wolves will not let us smoke or speak," said Young Snake. "Word was brought to us out of the hills. The Pawnees are on the warpath. Spotted Bull moves at their head. They are very many. Their horses are good and they count many rifles. They come straight toward our camp."

The chief smiled, and the expression was a dreadful grimace.

"When they come to us with guns and scalp knives," he said, "they are not coming against a squaw. Our men

4

are not children, and our boys are not girls. But these Pawnees are fools. I have heard that Spotted Bull is a wise chief. But does he think that the medicine of Thunder Moon has grown weak?"

"A hungry wolf," said Young Snake, "will try to pull down a bull moose. The Pawnees are hungry. Their scalps have been drying long over our fires. They have lost their honor and their name on the prairies. Men smile at the Pawnee nation. They are very hungry and they forget the medicine of Thunder Moon."

"Go to Thunder Moon, my friend," said the war chief. "Ask him if we shall draw out our fighting men. Perhaps he will take down fire from the Sky People and fling it in the faces of these fools, and then send them wandering and blind."

This pleasant thought made the eyes of Young Snake flash, as though in foretaste he already was ripping away the scalps of helpless men. There he left the teepee at once and crossed to an even larger one, whose skins were as white as snow and which had recently been painted with all of the skill that an Indian can show. Close beside it was another, much smaller lodge. At the entrance to the larger one he struck the board. A woman's shrill voice, quavering with age, bade him enter, and he stood just inside the threshold and looked about him with a good deal of awe.

To one side an ancient crone was rising. Her back was bowed with many years, but her long arms were still sinewy and strong. From beneath the folds of her eyelids bright, bird-like eyes peered at the stranger as she rose to greet a brave of her tribe.

"Thunder Moon is not here, White Crow?" he asked with a good deal of respect in his voice and in his manner. Indeed, he was like one treading upon sacred

5

ground.

"You come here with sweat on your face," said White Crow. "There is trouble for the Cheyennes again, and so they remember that I have a son in my lodge. Hungry dogs always have soft eyes when they smell food."

This bitter speech did not abash the warrior. He merely asked her if she could tell him where he could find her foster son.

"How should I tell you?" asked White Crow. "He sits by the river in a dream. The white devils have stolen his heart. Only a part of him is with the Cheyennes. Shall I tell you where to find him? Perhaps Red Wind will know."

He left the lodge and stood at the entrance of the smaller teepee, after casting one rather anxious glance through a gap among the tents and toward the open prairie in the direction from which the Pawnees might be expected. He dared not question the wisdom of the war leader, no matter how indifferent that hero might seem to be.

In answer to the blow of his hand on the entrance board, the flap of the teepee was pushed aside and, carrying in her hand the half-completed moccasin which she had been beading, Red Wind stood before the brave. Over one shoulder a great braid of copper-colored hair, looking as smooth and heavy as that metal in fact, dropped down even below her waist. But she had the dark skin and the dark eyes of an Indian. In twenty cities of white men, one might have hunted vainly to find another woman half so beautiful.

"Red Wind," said the warrior, "I have come to ask where I may find Thunder Moon. Where has he gone?"

Her face clouded at once. "How should I know?" she asked with some bitterness. "Does he live in my teepee?

Is he my husband? I am only a stranger who lives on his kindness. Why should he open his mind to me and tell me where he moves?"

She stepped back as though about to drop the flap of the teepee, then added coldly: "Go to Standing Antelope. He is more to Thunder Moon than all the other men among the Cheyennes. Go to him and ask him. He cannot fail to know the mind of the great warrior, by night or by day."

The flap of the teepee straightway fell and the brave remained for a moment, scowling, as though he was minded to call the girl back and teach her better manners. But he altered his mind and, turning, he strode rapidly through the village until he came to a much smaller lodge, in front of which sat a handsome young brave with such feathers in his hair as denoted feats done in battle in spite of his youth.

"Thunder Moon! Where is he?"

Standing Antelope frowned. "I do not carry him in my hand," he said. "How shall I tell? I only know where his mind is. In the land of his white fathers."

CHAPTER TWO

THE WISDOM OF THUNDER MOON

TO THE BLUNT ANSWER OF THE YOUTH YOUNG SNAKE, a hardened and seasoned brave, returned a baleful stare in which he surveyed the youngster from head to foot. Standing Antelope did not shrink from the survey, repaying it with a calmly insolent glance. Correction hesitated in the mind of the older man. It was true that Standing Antelope was young, but he was swift as the wind. He was not vastly experienced in life. On the other hand he had ridden on long forays at the side of Thunder Moon, and from that strange and terrible man he had learned gunplay with such skill that few among the Cheyennes would have been willing to stand against him.

Young Snake contained himself with saying: "A true friend should be as one's shadow."

With that he walked haughtily away, and plied his query again of a boy at the outskirts of the town, having remounted the chestnut mare in the first place. The boy had no hesitation at all. He pointed toward a clump of trees on the bank of the river, and toward this Young Snake galloped at full speed. He was growing nervous. It seemed to him, as he cast a glance over his shoulder at the wind-ruffled grass of the prairie, that the whole fate of the Cheyennes rested upon his activity. For what if the Pawnees should suddenly appear in a rushing charge?

He made the mare travel at high speed toward the designated clump of trees and, dismounting, he pressed through them and found Thunder Moon reclining at ease. Young Snake gazed upon that mighty form with awe. No tribe on all the plains possessed such power of hand as the Cheyennes and among all the Cheyennes there was no one to match the resistless force of Thunder Moon. Now, as he lay at ease, his strength appeared more formidable than in action. Hercules's striking is less suggestive of might than Hercules's leaning upon his club. In the hand of Thunder Moon lay a book, partly shaded by the down showering of his hair, cut short when he had lived among the whites, but now grown very long again. He brushed back this hair so that it fell more in order across his shoulders and nodded to Young Snake. Only at that hint did the messenger dare to speak.

"Thunder Moon," he said, "the Pawnees have been seen in force among the hills. They are going fast, and straight toward this camp it seems. Spotted Bull leads them"

"I am not the leader of the Cheyennes," said Thunder Moon. "This is a message for Bald Eagle."

"I have spoken to Bald Eagle. He told me to ask you if he should lead out the braves, or if you instead will go out and throw the fires of the Sky People in the faces of the Pawnees."

Thunder Moon thrust himself up on one arm. So doing, the buffalo robe which covered his shoulders dropped off and showed him, Indian fashion, naked to the waist and otherwise clad in trousers of the finest deerskin, heavily beaded in an intricate fashion.

"Am I," he said, "to be called upon every time the Pawnee dogs howl on the plains?"

Young Snake said diplomatically: "Battle is a small thing to Thunder Moon. He rides along through the country of the enemy. He sees them in crowds, their wise warriors and their brave young men, and he laughs. If he has need and so wishes, he calls upon the Sky People, and they send him help. They guide his bullets. They speak wisdom in his ear. We are not like you. It is true that we call the Pawnees wolves and dogs, but they are wolves and dogs that may bite!"

Thunder Moon closed his book with a reluctant sigh. He stood gathering into his hand a heavy cartridge belt which also supported at either side a long holster out of which the handles of revolvers appeared. This he buckled about his waist. From the tree beside him he took the long rifle which was leaning against it. Young

9

Snake, his dignity not impaired by waiting upon so eminent a warrior, picked up the fallen robe and threw it over the wide shoulders of Thunder Moon. Sun browned as they were, the naked flesh of the shoulders of Thunder Moon had showed clearly his white blood. Now that his body was covered he looked almost perfectly the part of an Indian for his hair was black and coarse, his eyes dark, and his face and throat were so bronzed that there were actually in the tribe paler complexions than his own. He had the face of an Indian, also—the wide, powerful jaw and the high cheekbones and the look of cruelty and decision, but perhaps there was more sensitive molding in his mouth and in the chiseling of his aquiline nose.

The rifle he carried in his left hand. In his right, he walked with a staff and so left the woods. Young Snake pointed to the mare.

"Will you ride?" he asked.

"While you walk?" asked Thunder Moon kindly. "No, brother. I have not loaned the mare to you in order to take her back the first time there is weariness in my feet."

They crossed the level stretch between the river and the village, Young Snake leading the mare behind him. As they went, a little crowd of boys swept down and swirled around them, like so many agile young birds on the wing. A boy of thirteen leaped before them, dancing backwards to keep out of their way.

"Is there war, Thunder Moon?" he asked cheerfully. "Is it true that the Pawnees are riding? If that is so, take me with you! I shall guard your back. No one shall come at you from behind. Take me with you, and I shall count one coup, or else may I die, and my scalp dry over a Pawnee fire."

10

"Boy," said Young Snake as reply, "have you learned the ways of men? Do you speak to a chief before he has spoken to you?"

He made a threatening gesture as he said this, but Thunder Moon merely smiled.

"What is your name?" he asked.

"I have no name!" cried the child. "I have sworn that I never shall take a name. I am nothing . . . until Thunder Moon sees me fighting, and then calls me what he pleases. He may call me anything, but he never shall have to say: 'Coward!' "

"Young fools boast and wise men smile," said Young Snake. "You raise a dust before us. Go away!"

"Go to my teepee," said Thunder Moon, still gently. "I shall give you an old rifle. Swear that you will not try to join a war party for a whole year. Go to Standing Antelope and he will teach you how to shoot. At the end of a year from this day . . . then we shall see how straight you can hold the rifle in your hands."

There was a wild yell of joy from the youngster. He leaped high into the air as though from a springboard, and then whirled and darted for the river to tell the swimming, wrestling, running boys there of the great prize which he had been promised.

Young Snake muttered: "You will turn all of our boys into beggars, Thunder Moon. Out of your hands good things flow faster than words out of the lips of other medicine men."

They entered the village. A young brave stepped suddenly beside them and raised a hand in greeting.

"Young man," said Thunder Moon's companion, "the chief is busy. He has no time for words with you."

"Are you in trouble?" asked Thunder Moon.

"I have a sore heart," said the other.

"Tell me, then, as we walk on."

"I am the unlucky man who married the daughter of Crooked Horn. I paid six good horses for her. She came to my lodge in the afternoon. She was gone by the night with another man. Now Crooked Horn refuses to give back my horses."

"He gave you his daughter," said Thunder Moon, "but he could not promise you the power to keep her. A thing that is done is ended. Where is the girl now?"

"They have gone back, I think, to the rest of the Suhtai. I only wait to settle my dispute with Crooked Horn before I follow them."

His face set; his nostrils expanded with savage resolution.

"Let them go," said Thunder Moon. "A woman who leaves one man will always leave two. She will cost her new lover horses, perhaps more than six, before he sees her for the last time."

"My empty lodge makes my heart very sick," said the brave.

"Then give away your lodge and all that is in it, except the weapons. Give the rest to the poor, and go to live with the other young men. Tell me . . . are you not the man who counted the coup on High Buffalo?"

"I am that man," said the youth. "Thunder Moon's eyes see all things, and in his mind he never forgets."

"When you ride on the war trail again," said Thunder Moon, "you shall ride at the side of Young Snake, here, upon one of my horses, if that will make you happier."

The youth could not speak. Joy choked him.

"Happy!" he cried at last, in a ringing voice. "This day I am born again! Thunder Moon, I shall give everything away. Since you have made me one of your men, I have better than a teepee of buffalo cowhide

12

because I have the whole sky for a lodge."

"As for the woman," said Thunder Moon, "it is best for you to think no more of her. If she had been a good woman, she would not have left you so soon after going to your teepee. Since she has proved herself to be a bad woman, why should you yearn for her? Does a man hunger for the thing that makes him sick?"

The young man went on, fairly reeling with joy.

"Once more! Once more!" said Young Snake. "The riches of the lodge of Thunder Moon are very great, but the riches of his wisdom are still greater."

Thunder Moon shook his head, with a faint smile.

"Ride through the camp and gather my men," he said. "We are going out to find those Pawnee wolves who dare to come so close to our city. That is to say, we shall ride out if Bald Eagle gives us his permission."

Young Snake whirled without a word, bounded upon the back of his horse, and hastily rode off through the camp. His face was illuminated with a confident joy, for the Cheyennes never took the dread of defeat with them when they rode out behind Thunder Moon. The latter had gone on into the teepee of Bald Eagle and briefly stated his purpose.

"Brother," said the war chief, "whatever your mind tells you to do is good. Shall I ride with you?"

"Only those who ride my horses are going," said Thunder Moon. "But you shall ride if you will."

"I stay here, then," said the chief. "Let the young men go out and gather the scalps of the dead men whom Thunder Moon leaves on the ground." He looked down as he spoke, for fear that the other would see the poisonous envy and hatred which at that moment was overflooding his soul.

13

CHAPTER THREE

TREACHERY

ALL MUSTERS WERE QUICKLY MADE IN THE INDIAN village. The followers of Thunder Moon rapidly assembled. He himself was cantering a horse among the teepees and encouraging his braves to hurry, until he came to the lodge of Standing Antelope. Here he called and, after a moment, the youth appeared at the entrance. A buffalo robe was gathered close about him. He appeared bowed, as if in pain or in weariness.

"The Pawnees!" called Thunder Moon. "Are you riding? Have they failed to bring you word?"

"Oh, my Father," said the young warrior, "there is hot pain in my heart. I don't think I could sit on the back of a horse. Besides, you do not need me. The finest braves follow you. Even without them, you could not fail. The Sky People ride at your side."

"When I come back," said Thunder Moon, "I shall see you again and then we shall talk about your sickness. Rest quietly and keep your mind cheerful. A sad mind makes a weak body, Standing Antelope."

He rode on. Standing Antelope stared gloomily after him. Then he retired to the quiet of his teepee. There he sat with the robe gathered around his head, trying to shut out the noises of celebration, the shouts of farewell and encouragement, as the braves gathered and departed on the war trail. His whole soul was on fire to join those riders who went out to hunt glory and to count coups, and he trembled with the passion for war. Yet he controlled himself and, for a long hour after the riders were gone, he waited. At last he got up and put on a suit of beaded deerskin.

He picked up a revolver but, remembering that this was a gift from Thunder Moon, he promptly laid it aside again. With only a knife at his belt and a staff in his hand, he walked out and went with dignity through the village. As the passage of a whirlwind leaves behind it circling little towers of dust, so the Cheyennes were gathered here and there in excited groups, discussing the war alarm. One seasoned brave, carried beyond himself, was prancing around and around in front of his lodge, like a rooster courting a hen and chanting a hideous war song. Standing Antelope went past this celebrant and came to the teepee of Red Wind. He spoke. She came to the entrance and smiled cheerfully on him.

He went close to her and said in a quiet voice: "He is gone, Red Wind. Let us go also. I have horses ready. Once we are away, he never will be able to find our trail."

She looked narrowly at him.

"Are you asking me to run away with you?" she asked bluntly.

He drew himself up.

"I am," he said.

"And why should I go?" asked Red Wind.

"My teepee is filled with wealth," he said. "I have fine backrests and many painted robes, and good pipes, and also pots and everything that a woman could wish, such as beads."

"Who gave you your wealth?" she asked.

"I fought for it," he said.

"You fought under the shield of Thunder Moon," said the girl.

"I have taken wounds in battle," he said. He pointed to a scar that seared his shoulder.

15

"Scratches," she said, "but Thunder Moon, with his medicine, has turned the bullets of the enemy away from you."

"Thunder Moon himself never will say so," he insisted.

"Because he is modest and he does not boast about the friendship of the Sky People."

"I have not only wealth," he said, "but I have wonderful swift horses."

"They are the red horses of Thunder Moon," she answered, "which he gave to you."

Standing Antelope struck the ground with his staff. "I have counted seven coups in battle!" he declared.

She answered: "You have counted your coups with Thunder Moon riding beside you, striking down every danger that came at you."

"You talk like a woman blind with love," replied Standing Antelope.

"Who, then, is greater than Thunder Moon?"

"Bah!" said the youth. "He never has passed the test. His heart was broken. It is said that he cried like a girl when his foster father would have tied the thongs in his flesh when he was a boy."

"It is very well for the Cheyennes to remember that day," murmured the girl. "He has saved them a thousand times in battle. Now they sneer at him."

"He never is brave, except when he knows that the Sky People are with him."

"Who rode into the land of the Comanches and took away their god, their Yellow Man . . . took it away from their own medicine lodge? The Comanches have had no good fortune since that day."

"A woman only looks with one eye and therefore how can she see the truth?" he replied. "Thunder Moon never

16

has taken a scalp."

"But he has counted more than thirty scalps . . . and in battle."

This testimony caused Standing Antelope to pause for a moment. Then he muttered: "It is true that the Sky People give him power. They make his heart bold, too. But why do you care so much for him?"

"Because he is the greatest and the bravest and the richest and the strongest chief among the Cheyennes!"

"He is not a chief," replied Standing Antelope. "Neither is he a medicine man."

"Whatever he is, he is himself," she said. "Who do the Pawnees fear? Who makes the Blackfoot tremble? Why do the Sioux leave the Cheyennes in peace?"

Standing Antelope bit his lip. Then he replied: "Of what use is a fine horse to the man who cannot sit on its back?"

"What do you mean by that?"

"You love Thunder Moon. Yet what are you to him?"

"Do you think," she answered angrily, "that I shall like you better because he likes me less?"

He said with emotion: "You do not know me, Red Wind. I am not old. But I am a man. Already I may speak in the council. The old men listen. Why will you not listen to me, Red Wind? You are nothing to Thunder Moon. He keeps you here out of his kindness. He is no Cheyenne. There is not a drop of Indian blood in his veins. I say that. You know it also. You have seen his father and his mother in the land of the white men. They despise us because of our red skins. So does he despise us!"

"He left his people and came back to us," she retorted.

"Because his people drove him out. He never has

17

smiled since that day. His heart is full of the memory of the white girl whom he left behind him."

It was the girl's turn to grow excited. She gripped both her hands hard and her breast heaved. "Thunder Moon takes what he wants, even out of the camp of the enemy," she said. "If he wanted the white girl, he would have taken her. You should know this."

"Among Indians, he is an Indian," answered Standing Antelope. "Among white men, he is a white. Among the whites, the word of a girl unstrings the arms of the strongest warriors. This I have seen, and you have seen it and know it also. You talk to make your own heart strong, but there is no strength and there is no truth in your words."

She stared at him, as though what he said had entered her heart deeply, and he went on: "Now you are sad and angry, because I have told you the truth. See what I offer to you in exchange. I am not a magician. I cannot call down the Sky People. I am not as rich as he. I have not a whole herd of such matchless horses as he inherited from Big Hard Face, who stole them from the whites . . . from Thunder Moon's own father. But I am a Cheyenne, and I am a man. I have passed the tests. I have had the thongs fastened deeply in my flesh, and I have dragged the buffalo skull until the thongs tore through the flesh and set me free to become a warrior. I have counted seven coups. I have taken five scalps. My gun shoots straight. I can strike hard with a lance. My knife is not dull. In the council I am not a fool. Also, I am young. If I have done something before, I shall do more hereafter. Besides, I love you. I have gone among the young women of the Cheyennes. They are no more to me than stars when the full moon is in the sky. I have ridden out on the war trail and fought hard, and gone hungry, and welcomed every pain because I hoped in that way I could drive away the thought of you."

"Standing Antelope," she said sternly, "how do you think that I may trust you? If you could betray a friend, would you be true to a woman?"

"I give up a friend whom I love for a woman whom I love still more," he said. "Besides, I have shown you that he will never make you his squaw. He has learned among the whites their ways of marriage. His wife would have to be a real wife, and one only, according to the ways of the whites. For the one woman, he already has made his choice."

Suddenly she drew her robe about her head. "Ah," she said, "you can break my heart, but you cannot take me away from him." She turned suddenly back into her lodge.

Standing Antelope went away with a pausing step. Bald Eagle, from before his own lodge, watched him going and motioned to him. The youth, half reluctantly, went to his chief.

"You have a sore heart?" said Bald Eagle.

"I am not happy," answered the brave.

"Patience, patience," said the war leader. "Patience will win the longest battle. Brave men know that the last blow is what decides the fighting."

The two looked fixedly upon one another with understanding, and then Standing Antelope resumed his way to his own lodge. It was a bitter day to him. Besides, it placed him in a quandary. He hardly could trust that Red Wind would not tell Thunder Moon of that conversation. If this were done, how could Standing Antelope remain in the camp without fighting against Thunder Moon? No matter how boldly he had spoken in the presence of the girl, he well knew in his heart of hearts that he could not stand for an instant before the strength and the skill of the white man.

He sat in his teepee and thought long thoughts. Twice he was on the verge of mounting his best horse and deserting the tribe, but always he resisted that temptation. He was so sick with love that he hardly cared how soon death came to him.

CHAPTER FOUR

TWO BRAVES MEET

ARMED TO THE TEETH, THUNDER MOON'S BAND OF chosen braves voyaged across the prairie. It was a sort of honorary troop which he had formed. He saw that every man was as perfectly armed as possible. Each carried a rifle of the best quality. Revolvers were of no use in their unfamiliar and inaccurate hands. But they had good knives, axes to fling at a short distance or use in hand-to-hand fighting, and long, slender lances, topped with the finest steel. Each, too, carried a shield of the toughest hide of the back of the buffalo bull—a substance so stout that often it stopped a spent bullet and still more often deflected a glancing one though, of course, it was of little use against rifle fire well aimed and at a reasonable range. It would, however, serve as a defence against hand-flung missiles, and against axe stroke or lance thrust. All of the score of warriors who followed Thunder Moon were armed in this fashion. They set off their weapons and their defensive arms with a fluttering host of feathers and many a pound of bright beads, so that the party flashed and glistened almost like ancient knights in armor, crossing the plains.

Though they had been carefully trained by Thunder Moon in the proper and accurate use of the rifle, their chief strength lay in their horses. First stolen from the herd of Sutton on that distant day by Big Hard Face, the foster father of Thunder Moon, the original nucleus had increased to two score animals, old and young, and nothing that trod the plains could be compared with them. It gave them over other warriors on the prairies the same advantage that fast ships had over less weatherly enemies—that is to say, they could stand down for battle when they chose, weaker parties could not escape from them, and overwhelming numbers they always could flee. Many a time the force of these advantages had been proved. With a keen and restless confidence the warriors now followed their leader. They looked upon him almost as a god, convinced of his invincibility in war.

In two hours they put the camp well behind them and they had broken into the region of higher hills when the advance guard whirled and raced back. He had seen the Pawnees. They were coming straight up the valley— nearly five score warriors, well armed and mounted as the first report had accurately stated.

Thunder Moon ordered his men to dismount. He concealed them in the long grass of a hilltop, leaving three men in the rear to handle the horses and keep them in readiness for a retreat. When this was done, he rode boldly out into the valley in full view of the advancing Pawnees. It was his hope to draw them straight past his concealed force which then could pour in a searching fire and make away to their horses and escape before the pursuit became effective.

Upon a little swell of ground in the midst of the valley he took his post and watched the irregular body of the Pawnees jogging toward him. Nearly every warrior appeared to carry a rifle. In the rear a large herd of horses was being brought on by several Pawnee boys.

Coming still closer, the Pawnees suddenly seemed to recognize an enemy. They flogged their horses into a gallop and bore down upon the lone horseman at a terrific speed. Still he did not move from his position, though some of the enemy already had unlimbered their rifles and were firing. The distance was still too great for any sort of accuracy.

The bullets, in fact, were fired by those who realized that they were mounted on slow horses and, therefore, could not get up to the battle in time to do execution on the stranger, except with a chance, long-range shot. Thunder Moon watched that charge with a grim satisfaction. He was just about to twitch his stallion around and send him flying to the rear when he saw a chief break forward through the mass of the Pawnees and begin to make many violent gestures, shouting.

A great war chief of the Pawnees, perhaps, encouraging his men to the charge! He saw that the warriors were restrained on either hand. Their pace became slower. Suddenly the whole body halted at the front, those in the rear bringing up their ponies and then stopping so as to form a fairly dense line.

The leader, in the meantime, advanced by himself and signaled with sign language from a distance that he wished to converse with the solitary rider. Thunder Moon, nothing loathe, advanced in turn. They met in the midst of the valley. Thunder Moon saw before him a stocky, powerful man of middle age or a little less, with a particularly gross and brutal face.

It was Spotted Bull, a famous and lucky hero among the Pawnees, particularly distinguished for raids in which he had driven off horses from the Cheyennes, the Blackfoot, and even from the Sioux themselves—a tribe which, on account of its great numbers, most of the other plains warriors were glad to leave alone.

This chief came straight up to Thunder Moon, his rifle in its case, his shield slung over his shoulder, and only his long, light lance in his hand. Even this he did not carry on clear to the point of meeting, but jabbed the butt of it into the ground and rode on empty-handed to the meeting. He raised a hand in greeting.

He said to Thunder Moon with much complacency: "Now that two such famous chiefs have met, Thunder Moon, let me know why we should not part as friends?"

"What friendship has there ever been between the Cheyennes and the Pawnees?" asked Thunder Moon sternly.

The other was undisturbed. "No doubt," he said, "we are generally at war with one another, but that is no reason why there should not be peace, now and again. What are you to gain today from me? No doubt you have some of your men hidden nearby, watching with their rifles. Probably you have not so many as I. Even suppose that the Sky People guide your bullets and kill some of us from a distance, still you are not apt to do us much harm. If you take any of our blood, then we must try to have vengeance, and that would mean for many days your village would be very uncomfortable. Men are not happy when they are surrounded with stinging bees, and the Cheyennes do not sleep soundly when they hear the wolves howling in the night."

At the aptness of this remark, Thunder Moon could not help smiling a little.

"On the other hand," went on Spotted Bull, "it is very hard to find any honor from Thunder Moon. All the nations of the plains know that very well. Now I wish to say to you that we have not ridden out to do any harm to the Cheyennes. We do not wish to strike at your young men. We have enough horses to carry us very well without trying to steal some of yours . . . ."

Here his eye could not help glistening with hunger as he looked at the mighty stallion which Thunder Moon bestrode.

"We have another goal, brother," concluded Spotted Bull. "That is why I offer that we should all be friends for a few days. My brother is wise. He knows that it is easy to snuff out the flame of life in a brave warrior. Yet it is not easy to raise another in his place."

The leader of the Cheyennes nodded. "Everything that you say is true," he said. "If we have not had peace in the past, it is no very good reason why we should not have peace for a time now. I am not the war chief of the Cheyennes in this village. A great warrior, Bald Eagle, leads us."

"Bald Eagle has that honor of being war chief but," said the Pawnee, with a flattering frankness, "if it were only for Bald Eagle, perhaps we should not be so anxious to have peace with the Cheyennes just now. It is Thunder Moon whom we know very well. We have seen his hand striking. Also, I know that when he speaks, all of the Cheyennes listen. Let me have your promise to speak for us. After that I shall care nothing."

This flattery touched Thunder Moon sufficiently to make him answer: "Spotted Bull, you speak very kindly. Kindness from a stranger makes the brain sleep. I shall try to do what you want. If you are not riding into our country in order to make war on us, what is it that you wish to do, and where are you going?"

"A good rifle is best kept in one holster," said the

cunning Pawnee, "and a secret is safest when it is lying in one mind. But to a famous man I must give an answer. Is it not true, Thunder Moon, that not very long ago you went to live among the whites for a time?"

"That is true."

"And that you left them?"

"Yes."

"That in fact they hunted you out?"

The frown of Thunder Moon was a sufficient answer.

"These things are talked of among all the tribes on the plains," said Spotted Bull. "The Pawnees," he added with additional flattery, "were so unhappy when they heard that Thunder Moon had gone. They were not very glad when they learned that he had come back again to the Cheyennes. But I know that after such a thing has happened, you have no great love in your heart for the whites?"

"If a dog is kicked," said Thunder Moon, in oblique answer, "he licks the hand of his master who beat him. If a wolf is struck, he leaps at the throat."

"So!" said the Pawnee chief, "Thunder Moon will teach the white men that they were fools to throw him out. This I can understand. It could not be any other way that a man would act. Then I freely tell you that I was riding against the whites."

"That will be a great war," answered Thunder Moon. "I have been in their country, brother. I know the numbers of their warriors. Since we are speaking as friends, I tell you the truth."

"I am not riding against their towns," answered the Pawnee. "But they have sent out a party into the plains. That party has killed a Pawnee. It is right that they all should die like dogs and that we should take their scalps, their horses, and their weapons!" He added: "It is said that they have very fleet horses, but I think that they cannot run as fast as the Pawnee bullets."

"You have told me the truth," said Thunder Moon. "I have nothing to say except to give you peace."

"Peace to you," answered Spotted Bull, "and to all of the Cheyennes. Afterward, we may meet in a different manner."

"The Sky People direct all things," said Thunder Moon, and frowned a little again.

"Here," said Spotted Bull, "is a shield that has kept my life safe twenty times. Three times it has turned away bullets from my heart. You see the marks upon it. Thunder Moon, take this shield, wear it in war, but not against the Pawnees. Let it be a sign that you are honored by your enemies!"

"Here is an axe," said Thunder Moon. "You see that the handle is all set over with rich beads. It is yours. It is a lucky axe. It has not saved lives, but it has taken two."

So they parted, and each rode back to his own men.

CHAPTER FIVE

GRAY BEAR

OUT OF THE GRASS AROSE THE TWENTY CHEYENNES, took their twenty horses, and sat in the wind, their feathers blown sheer back upon their heads, watching the Pawnees—those ancient, traditional enemies—ride slowly past them into the heart of the valley. They looked down to the unharmed Pawnees; they looked without regarding the greater numbers. For they were invincible, they felt. They were the men of Thunder Moon, who would not know defeat. They looked to the

26

foe, and then they looked to their leader and their faces grew darker.

All the Pawnees went past. They went in a silence, like the silence of guilty apprehension, until the Cheyennes ground their teeth. The longer the Pawnees marched upon their small ponies, quietly past, the more powerful and secure they felt themselves. They saw beneath them four score honorable scalps growing upon Pawnee heads, and their hands clasped the handles of their knives and they rolled eyes of agony upon one another.

Then the enemy departed through the hills, rising and dipping like a ship through green seas, streaming soon out of sight.

"Suppose that they turn and ride for the village?" asked one gloomy warrior. "Suppose that they are riding now with all their might, now that we cannot see them any longer?"

Thunder Moon said: "If we had fought, we would have killed some of them. They would have killed some of us. The speed of our horses would not have saved us altogether. Horses cannot run faster than bullets. I never have heard a truer thing said than that. I would not kill twenty Pawnees at the cost of five Cheyennes!"

So he spoke, but one of the younger braves muttered, no louder than a whisper: "That is what he says to us now, when his blood is cool. But let his blood get hot and he would throw us all away for the sake of fight. Thunder Moon perhaps has lost the support of the Sky People. Perhaps they no longer hear him speak."

So he said. Eyes widened with fear at the mere thought. There was malice, too, in their faces. Thunder Moon, though he did not hear that malicious voice, plainly understood the meaning of those expressions.

But he did not heed them. He had known for years the quality of having divine or semi-divine powers attributed to him. Impossibilities were asked of him. If he did not undertake them with a smile, then it was because he was lazy and cruel, or else because he had lost his powers. Or again, if the slightest thing turned out well, it was not because of his own brain and the strength of his own mind, as it was because of the Sky People.

He hardly knew what he felt about them now—those dim beings of the upper world. There had been a day when he would have shuddered at the mere thought of doubting their existence, but now he altered somewhat, having lived for long, long months among the white men of his own kin. He could not help remembering the books which invaded the marvels of the sky and made the rain and the blowing of the winds all seem normal and natural things, not attributable to the wrath or the pleasure of the spirits, but entirely to the physical powers of the sun which lifts the waters from the ocean and causes all the weight of the winds to blow.

Yonder, over the mountains, where the rivers run down to the eastern sea, it was easy enough to give credence to the spirit of science. Not so easy upon the broad breast of the prairie which, with mysterious curve, presses man up closer to the wild bosom of the sky. Though his mind would often say no, yet in great moments his instinct and all his heart made him look upwards for help as he had done so many times, all his life. He had not actually prayed to the Sky People for these many, many months. For this, even, he felt more and more guilty. Perhaps they had turned their backs upon him. So he understood perfectly the shadow that ran over the faces of his men, like a cloud shadow

28

running over a group of hills.

His thought turned back to the last thing which had disturbed him. The Pawnees rode to attack the whites. Somewhere they would strike the wanderers and wipe them out perhaps. He was amazed and troubled by the thought. Amazed to know that it could pain him so deeply, when he remembered how those of his own color, his own blood, had driven him out with bullets!

Then he called forth Young Snake. There was hardly a better or a more seasoned warrior in his entire band.

He said: "Go back with the other men to the village of the Cheyennes. I am riding alone."

Young Snake looked upon his master with a burning and a hungry eye.

"Oh, Thunder Moon," he said at last, in a voice that actually quivered, "I hear you and I understand. There is no longer glory for Thunder Moon in striking the enemy with so many followers. He wants to go alone, his guns speaking, and the Pawnees falling. He wants to count twenty coups in a single battle. But think of us. We follow you for the sake of glory!"

Thunder Moon could not help smiling a little as he answered: "Do you think that I would attack them single handed, one man against eighty? Is that a wise man's thought, Young Snake?"

Young Snake answered with a perfect devotion: "What are many enemies to you, oh, Thunder Moon?" He explained himself with the most cheerful of smiles: "When the Sky People ride with you, do they count the number of the faces of the Pawnees before them?"

The big man answered briefly: "The Sky People bid me to ride alone, and not for the sake of a battle. I have told you what to do. Ride back to the village. I will not change my mind."

At this direct command, Young Snake obediently drew off. The other warriors sulkily heard his voice, and suddenly they fled across the hills on the homeward trail, like so many shadows mounted upon red streaks, so rapidly did the big chestnuts run.

Thunder Moon rode on alone, and with the greatest caution, upon the trail of the Pawnees. He knew that there was need of every care. No matter how friendly Spotted Bull might be when Thunder Moon appeared with a band of practiced warriors at his back, all mounted upon those most dreaded, those most desired coursers, nothing was clearer than that the Pawnee chief would break ten thousand promises, would break them in a very ecstasy of delight, so that he could have the joy of taking or slaying Thunder Moon, that fire-brand, that bolt from heaven, lodged in the hands of the lucky Cheyennes.

So Thunder Moon went on cautiously, his care redoubled because he knew his own deficiencies upon the trail. It was well enough when he voyaged across the plains with some of the most expert trailers of the Cheyenne nation to guide him aright, to spread out before and behind to catch the very first signals of danger. It was another matter when he had to make such a journey alone.

Even an Indian woman, even an Indian child, had sharper eyes than his, had quicker senses to note the changes upon the grass, the leaves, the ground, which indicated that other life stirred nearby. By the flight of the very birds, they could read what was passing along the surface of the earth, many miles away, and yet all of these abilities were quite beyond the talents of Thunder Moon.

Certainly though he went, he knew that he was

overtaking the Indian column. The walk of the big stallion was equal to the jog of the Indian ponies, and the trot of the chestnut was the equivalent of a mustang's canter; whereas the long-striding gallop had no counterpart among the hobbling, broken gaits of the prairie horses.

There was no dust cloud ahead to show him the nearness of the Pawnees. He could tell, in a way, by the manner in which the bent and trampled grasses were coiling upwards again, the heads still moving. Twice, therefore, he halted. Twice he started onward with the keenest caution, knowing that such a wise chief as Spotted Bull was not apt to trust to an informal treaty of peace such as had just been completed, but would surely throw out rear guards to spy against any possible surprise attack.

He came to a narrow little gorge where a stream wound back and forth through the flat, pebbly bottom. He went down this, where the grass grew so tall that it brushed against the feet of Thunder Moon. The sun glittered like the flashing of steel blades on the polished surface of the grass, like the flashing of steel blades but not quite like the dull sheen of a rifle-barrel.

Thunder Moon whirled in the saddle as the rifle jumped to the shoulder of the Pawnee. He saw a hideous face, streaked with war paint, and he flung the heavy bull-hide shield from his left arm straight at the Indian.

The rifle spoke. The shield staggered to its course and fell to the ground as the bullet ripped sidewise through it. It would have been easy to finish off the man with a bullet from his revolver, but Thunder Moon was full of the white man's fighting madness such as never comes over a savage brain. The Indian fights as coolly as a wild beast—he always avoids risks if he can. Twenty

31

men will not press home a charge against three, if the rifles of the three are loaded. But the white man rejoices in a sort of drunken, berserk lust of battle for battle's sake. He marches willingly behind the banner of a lost cause; and with a cheerful mind he volunteers for the most desperate hazard. So Thunder Moon followed his flung shield with a leap like a catamount that drove him from the back of his horse and straight upon the Pawnee.

It was a practiced and wide-shouldered warrior, bull-necked, cunning of hand, with an arm of iron. But he could not stand against the charge of Thunder Moon. He had dropped his rifle and caught out his knife just as the weight of the white man smashed into him and bore him heavily to the ground.

Kneeling beside him, Thunder Moon watched the stunned victim gradually open his eyes. He made no further attempt at resistance. Blankly he gazed up at the leader of the Cheyennes, and waited for death. Thunder Moon gathered to his hand the knife, the hatchet, the rifle of the Pawnee.

"The Pawnees keep good treaties and their word is sacred," said Thunder Moon bitterly. "Hardly two hours have passed since I made friendship gifts to your chief and received the same from him. Here is a wolf in my path, jumping at my throat."

The warrior did not attempt an answer.

"Rise!" said Thunder Moon.

The Pawnee rose to his feet.

"Is there any reason why I should not send a bullet through your brain?"

"Dog of a Cheyenne!" answered the Pawnee with a dauntless heart. "The Sky People turned my bullet aside from your heart. Or else you would lie dead here, and tonight I should be a great man among my people. Kill me as you please. I am not sorry that I tried to end your days."

"What is your name?"

"It is known to my people."

"I can tell you," said Thunder Moon, "by the scars across your shoulder. You are Gray Bear, are you not?"

At this the discretion of the Pawnee could not prevent a flash of pleasure from appearing in his eyes.

"A man will be known even in the lodges of his enemies," he said. "A great warrior is named in the camps of the foemen! I am Gray Bear."

"You have taken Cheyenne scalps, Gray Bear."

"I have taken three Cheyenne scalps. One from a man, one from a woman, one from a child. Even you, Thunder Moon, cannot kill me three times. Not even all the skill of the Sky People could teach you how to do that!"

"Where is your horse?"

"He is near."

"Show him to me."

The Pawnee whistled. A pony sprang up from the grass and came forward.

"Your horse knows you," said Thunder Moon. "Get on his back. Ride on with me."

The Pawnee obeyed without a word, but a settled sternness of gloom appeared on his face, as though he were seeing, long beforehand, the burning fire in the Cheyenne camp where the women would torment him to death.

They journeyed on to the brow of the rising land. As their heads came up across the top of the grass, they could see in the distance the moving line of the Pawnees, with the sun winking upon the bright tips of their spears.

The prisoner sighed, ever so slightly, and Thunder Moon said to him: "Keep close to my side. Ride slowly. All may be better for you than you imagine."

CHAPTER SIX

ATTACK

THE PROBLEM OF THUNDER MOON WAS NOW considerably complicated. He had to watch a strong and capable warrior at his side—even if that man were disarmed—quite likely to undertake any desperate and sudden attack upon him. In addition, he had to look out for other rear guards who might have been thrown out to watch.

For some time they journeyed on, having cautious sight now and again of the Pawnees who traveled before them over the top of some grass-grown hummock upon the prairie. There were no further encounters with subtle watchers who lay in the grass.

While they rode on, the mind of Thunder Moon turned somewhat between the dangers which beset him and the glory which he already had won upon this expedition. To take a scalp was most brave and admirable—but not a scalp had he ever taken. Inward repugnance could not be overcome in that direction. To slay in battle was a great deed. To count a coup was yet more worthy. But best of all was it to carry into the village of the Cheyennes a prisoner and, of all prisoners, who so welcome as a grown and famous warrior? The women had a thousand wrongs and remembered deaths to avenge. They would expiate them upon the person of this brave. The grim face of Gray Bear already acknowledged his approaching fate.

Another thought, too, interfered with the mind of Thunder Moon. He could not help remembering that the whites among whom his kin lived would never have acted thus toward a prisoner. A defenseless man was not to be harmed physically. He might be imposed upon, but his life was sacred.

This new standard troubled Thunder Moon and made him scowl askance at the Pawnee. Then, almost against his will, he looked up and was aware of a small white cloud sailing across the upper heavens, filled with radiance, as though the sun were seated in its center.

"The Sky People," he thought inwardly. No matter how little he consciously believed in that old superstition, in spite of himself he was comforted and reassured.

They came up behind another hummock and Thunder Moon suddenly reined back his horse, for he had had a view of the line of the Pawnees crouched behind a low ridge just before him, their horses held further down the slope. Beyond, across the prairie, came a stream of wagons. More than a score, he guessed them to be, plodding one behind the other through the rich sea of grass.

Sheltered from view once more, he said to Gray Bear: "Spotted Bull rides to attack those wagons?"

The answer of the Pawnee was indirect, but from the heart: "May he take many scalps! May he cover the wagons with blood! May he take some of them to kill afterwards, little by little!"

"Why do you hate the whites?" asked Thunder Moon. "Have they killed a son or a brother of yours?"

"No."

35

"Have they carried off any of your horses or a squaw?"

"What are women and horses?" said the Pawnee with contempt. "They may be taken again from enemies. The Blackfoot, the Sioux, and the Cheyennes," he declared with a glance of defiance at Thunder Moon, "raise the horses which the Pawnee wolves will ride! It is not for that that I hate them."

"For what reason, then?"

"Because they do not believe in our spirits, they do not fight in our ways, and they do not live by our customs. Why should you ask reasons for hating the white man, have they not driven you out? Yet your skin is white, also."

This answer effectively silenced Thunder Moon and made him look bitterly on his captive. He could understand the taunts, open or implied, of the Pawnee. They were aimed at rousing in him such a furious and headstrong anger that a bullet or a knife stroke would quietly and more fully end the life of Gray Bear and thereby save him from the hands of the Cheyenne women.

He did not answer, but now, by degrees, they both worked up again to the edge of the ridge and looked over on the scene which was developing. The Pawnees kept the same position, except that a band of a dozen, to the right, were moving down the hollow on their horses as though to be prepared to make a flank attack.

In the meantime the wagon train came closer and closer, moving with a sort of assured slowness, like a force conscious of its own strength and calmly despising all danger.

There were fully twenty of the big canvas-covered schooners, drawn by teams of oxen, a little gap between the rear of one wagon, and the horns of the following cattle. With their clumsy but powerful steps they pushed on through the prairie. Around the train rode horsemen, three or four in front, and others to either side. It seemed that they rode for pleasure and comfort rather than to keep guard, for otherwise they should have been pushed out to ten times such a distance, so as to act as spies in the treacherous Indian country.

The leading wagons had begun to mount a slight rise. The wind was dead. In the mortal stillness, Thunder Moon could hear the creaking of the great wheels upon their axles and, dimly, the shouts of the ox drivers as they used their goads freely. For this train was long out from the settlements, and the cattle were weary—soft with such lush green fodder and weak with the long days of labor.

Those dim voices, like thoughts rather than physical facts, haunted Thunder Moon with a strange sadness. He suddenly saw the house of his father, and the big white walls flooded with sunshine and with showers of green climbing vines. He heard the Negroes singing in the fields. He looked through a window of his heart and saw his mother in the stately library, her needlework in her lap.

What thoughts had she of him since they had driven him back to the wilderness and the wild people?

A rifle shot cracked from the hollow before him. He saw the long line of the Pawnees break over the crest of the low ridge and pour with the most fearful yells across the level, brandishing their spears, shaking their rifles above their heads.

"Ha," grunted Gray Bear. "They will swallow those white men. They will take the cattle, and the horses, and the guns, and the whiskey, too. There will be much firewater among so many wagons. All is ours!"

For the moment he had forgotten that he was himself a wretched captive, that the most unlucky white man in that train was hardly to be pitied more than himself.

The wagon train, threatened so suddenly on the plains, instantly began to act. The leading wagons turned sharply around and began to move toward the rear, while the frantic, yelling drivers goaded the oxen to a trot, then to an inconceivably heavy, lumbering gallop.

While the head of the train turned back in this fashion, the rear likewise curled about to join the front. The purpose, of course, was to form the wagons into some sort of a rough circle, from which, as from the walls of a fort, the riflemen could keep up a steady fire and drive the enemy away.

Slowly, slowly moved the wagons. The Pawnees rode on wings to strike. Gray Bear groaned with eagerness and with joy as he saw the probable success of the charge.

There were brave and ready men in that caravan, and the rifles worked steadily. Three of the red riders were knocked out of their saddles, but the rest rode on, lying flat along the backs of their ponies, and screeching like so many devils.

The head and tail of the caravan, gradually nearing, now seemed to have an equal chance of actually locking, when a bullet fired by one of the Pawnees struck a bullock which was struggling forward in the lead team from the rear. The animal dropped, dragged in the yoke, and then the wagon slewed around to the side.

It was only possible to close the gap at this point by having the wagon next following veer outside the one which had been checked. But the driver of the second

38

wagon, utterly confused, merely halted when the one before him was checked. It was the old habit of following the leader which all the drivers soon learned upon the prairie.

In this case it proved fatal. The progress from the rear being stopped, the whole caravan looked a helpless thing, like a hedgehog which quite fails to curl up before the reaching paw of the lynx rips up its belly. But he who drove the lead wagon was a man of sense. Seeing that he could not join the rearmost ox team, he turned in almost at right angles to the left, and the other wagons streamed after him, thus striving to close up a smaller circle which would protect at least a portion of the entire line.

Now into the open gap the Pawnees streamed, screeching like mountain lions over a kill. They rode erect, firing to either side. But they had divided their attention; some turned on the nearly defenseless wagons to the rear. Some raced on to try to prevent the front half of the train from closing up. The latter were foiled, and Thunder Moon saw them recoil as the circle was completed.

CHAPTER SEVEN

"WHO ARE YOU?"

WELL SHELTERED BEHIND THE WAGONS, THE MEN OF the circle maintained a steady fire against the Pawnees, but the latter now had a similar shelter. They swept in a single rapid wave over the remainder of the wagons. Wild cries of agony and wilder cries of triumph went up to heaven, and then the Indians threw themselves into position behind the captured wagons to open fire upon those which remained. After the first few moments, seeing that they were making only a small impression upon the remainder of the white fighters, they gave the greater part of their attention to the looting of the train in their hands.

The wind was dead. A thin smoke cloud from the firing of many rifles began to sway out and envelop the battle. Thunder Moon turned to his captive.

He had come with a bland satisfaction to see the wiping out of the whites. He found in his heart an increasing rage. Under his glare, the Pawnee chief winced, but Thunder Moon merely said to him: "You are free. Go back to Spotted Bull. Tell him that our truce is ended. He has counted many coups and taken many scalps. His hands are heavy with plunder. Tell him to guard himself: the Cheyennes are on his trail."

The Pawnee did not wait to be reassured. He gave merely one incredulous glance to his captor, then he sent his pony off at a jog trot. When he was a hundred yards away, as though suddenly mastered by fear, he put the whip to his horse and shot off in rapid zigzags across the grass, like a snipe flying upwind. Thunder Moon grimly watched him go. Bitterly he wished for those chosen warriors whom he had sent back under Young Snake.

He turned the tall stallion and drove at full speed back toward the Cheyenne village. In less than an hour, he sighted the smoke above the teepees, then the village itself. His horse was tramping through the water of the little river. He sent his shout before him and the whole town roused itself in answer. As he came up, Young Snake was the first to gallop out to greet him, armed at all points. Behind him streamed the rest of Thunder

Moon's own private band of adherents. Other volunteers young and old, eager to take the warpath behind so famous and lucky a leader, galloped in pursuit. Thunder Moon waited for no more. With that advance guard of proved and well-equipped warriors, he headed across the prairie. He did not follow the straight line toward the scene of the recent battle and slaughter of the whites. Instead, he cut off at right angles to that line of march. He reasoned that it would be very strange if Spotted Bull should remain to exult on the field of the battle after the warning that he had received through the liberated captive. He was more apt to take the first and the quickest trail toward his homeland.

If he moved to the left, it was very likely that Thunder Moon would cross that line of march. If he moved to the right, he would be free. With one chance in two to gamble for, Thunder Moon drove his men remorselessly. Even those fine horses on which he had mounted his chosen men—the wealth of his dead foster father and his own glory—were now punished relentlessly forward while the others, mounted on the Indian ponies, lagged to the rear in spite of all that whip and club could do to punish them forward.

Ten miles of prairie rolled behind them, and then a youth scouting ahead whirled back to announce that there was visible in the distance a column of riders, coming straight toward them at a round pace. Thunder Moon himself pushed forward and swung to his eyes the glass which he always carried. Instantly he recognized the Pawnees by their cropped heads. Behind the file of warriors came the herd of horses, mixed with the cattle recently taken from the wagons of the whites. A foolish move for Spotted Bull to have taken such slow moving animals if he wished to move with celerity.

41

There was no doubt about his haste. He had pushed out to either side two or three scouts to ride in advance. The line came on with gaps in it, showing that some of the horses were being distanced by the rest.

Not Indians alone rode in that procession. The very first thing that Thunder Moon saw—more moving to him than the flashing of a sword—was the long waving of a woman's hair. Then he made out the bundle of an infant in her arms, two children riding one behind another on another horse and, upon a third a man evidently wounded or broken hearted, for his head was sunk upon his breast.

Thunder Moon smiled, and the smile was not good to see. His own dispositions were easily made. The horses were swept back into a sunlit hollow. The riders were thrown forward into the high grass along the ridge of a knoll which was rather a small wave of green than a hill. In a moment the Cheyennes were out of view, peering out through the grass blades at the procession of the Pawnees.

In a murmur Thunder Moon passed his word among his warriors—to everyone who recaptured alive one of the white captives of the Pawnees there would go in full and free possession one of the chestnut horses. It was a gift worth the risking of life!

In the meantime it appeared as though this stratagem would be wasted. Far distanced by the ride of Thunder Moon's band across the prairie, a score of Cheyennes on their war ponies had clung to the trail and now these were in plain sight, coming rapidly on.

Spotted Bull must have sighted them at the same time. Some thirty of his own warriors were dispatched to the side to confront this strange menace but, though he deployed across the line of the Cheyenne approach, still the out-numbered Cheyennes came on. They well knew that somewhere in the sea of the tall grass, Thunder Moon and his chosen warriors were placed.

The Pawnees on the other hand, as though amazed by this resolute advance, wavered a little, uncertain. Spotted Bull himself, with half a dozen of his best warriors, rode out to reinforce his advance guard while his main body, now reduced by half, came slowly on with the captives.

All was working out for the best interests of the Cheyennes. The late comers from the village bore straight on against Spotted Bull. Just behind that chief lay Thunder Moon and his chosen fighters in the grass; and straight toward the concealed line came on the rest of the Pawnees. One Pawnee division was already tacitly taken from the rear; the others would be swept with surprise.

To the left, from Spotted Bull's immediate adherents, a rifle cracked and then another, but Thunder Moon, half rising to his knees, saw with joy that the Cheyennes kept on their rapid advance, merely fanning out their line so as to offer poorer targets. The head of the Pawnee main body was jogging close and closer. A dozen yards from Thunder Moon's concealed warriors —and then, silently—the Cheyennes rose to their knees in the grass and, with a deliberate aim, they blew the head of the column to bits.

The sudden blast of more than twenty well-aimed rifles took the Pawnees so completely by surprise that it was as though the ground before them had opened and spat forth fire and destruction into their defences. They rolled back in utter confusion. The Cheyennes leaped in among them with clubbed rifles, with knives, and with thrusting narrow-headed lances.

Thunder Moon, his rifle cast aside, a revolver in either hand made at the woman and saw her Pawnee guard whirl on her with lifted hatchet. Two quick shots dropped the guard. Thunder Moon stood at the head of the horse and looked up into a white, drawn, bewildered face, and saw trembling hands that clutched the infant closer.

"Have courage," he said rapidly to her. "You are safe. No one will harm you."

He turned back to the battle; but it was ended already. The men with Spotted Bull, amazed and unnerved by the eruption of rifleshots immediately behind them and with a rush of Cheyennes pouring toward them, did not even pause to discharge their rifles, but turned and fled. As they turned, the riders on the Cheyenne ponies whipped vigorously in pursuit. Woe to the Pawnee whose horse stumbled or proved a laggard!

The tall chestnuts, rushed up from their hiding place in the hollow, were hastily mounted. They darted away to join the pursuit, their long strides rapidly overtaking the fugitives. In another instant the sounds of battle were scattered far across the prairie and in all directions. Here was a Cheyenne group busy taking scalps. Others rounded up the herd of cattle and horses. Others took the fallen plunder. Still the greater part were scouring the plains east and north and south and west to count fresh coups and hunt down the traditional enemy.

It was as great a stroke as Thunder Moon himself ever had delivered. Yet he felt no keen pleasure as he looked on the work which was still under way. It seemed to him, with a stabbing suddenness of truth, that the death of one white, even woman or child, was more than enough to counterbalance all the vengeance which he could execute upon the entire Pawnee nation.

Bitterly he realized this. He had been cast out from

among his people. He knew in full what they meant to him and that an Indian name and an Indian life never could give him an Indian's heart.

The white fugitives were gathered in a close cluster, surrounded by half a dozen braves who were disputing as to which actually had rescued them—a problem which Thunder Moon himself had to solve. The two children and the woman who carried the infant were half hysterical with joy and with relief. He had them placed on the ground to rest and steady their nerves. He turned to the white man and found, as he had expected, that the latter had been wounded, a rifle ball having passed through his left thigh so that it had been a constant agony for him to remain in the saddle.

With all the skill which he had learned from whites and Indians, Thunder Moon cut open the trouser leg and cleansed and dressed the wound. A swallow of whiskey out of a flask restored the color to the face of the sufferer and he said quietly: "God knows what luck sent you here at the right moment. But if you had come a few hours before, you would have saved a horrible massacre."

"I saw the attack," said Thunder Moon. "Tell me. Did the last circle of the wagons hold? Or did the damned Pawnees break through and slaughter them, too?"

"No, they beat the Pawnees off. You . . . ." He paused, looking earnestly at Thunder Moon. "Do you know me?" he asked.

"I?" said Thunder Moon. "Certainly not."

"Will you tell me who you are?"

"I am a Cheyenne. They call me Thunder Moon."

"By heaven," said the other, "I thought so! Your hair was shorter when I last saw you, and you were not so sun browned, but you are William Sutton."

CHAPTER EIGHT

WHAT THE SKY PEOPLE DID

TO THIS RECOGNITION THUNDER MOON REPLIED IN THE uttermost astonishment: "Who are you? Where have you seen me?"

"I'm Charles Siegler," said the other, "and I used to see you near your father's place. I had the small farm down the road with the row of poplars in front of it and the pool beside the trees. Do you remember me, sir?"

Thunder Moon closed his eyes. He remembered very well the tall, slender, graceful trees, and their images ever afloat on the surface of the little lake.

"I remember you, Siegler. I remember you very well," he said. "No doubt you were one of the men who hounded me out of the country with guns and dogs? Were you one of those?"

"No, sir, I thank God!" said the other with violence. "I had nothing to do with that bad day's work."

"Bad day?" said Thunder Moon darkly. "Was it a bad day's work to hunt down a murderer?"

"Murderer?"

"There were dead men in the jail behind me."

"Ah, and was that it?" asked Siegler. "As a matter of fact there were no dead men at all, and he who hounded the others after you knew it very well. No, sir, since your leaving there was never a time when a great many people did not make a stir about bringing you back. Your father and mother have gone to the expense of fitting up the wagons and the cattle to go across the prairies and find you."

"To find me!" cried Thunder Moon. "How many died

when the Pawnees rushed the train?"

"I saw five men down, and three women, and three children," said Charles Siegler.

"Eleven dead," muttered Thunder Moon. "But why in the name of my father's God did he send out women and children to help hunt for me?"

"Those were not all his men," answered Siegler. "We fell in with another small train. We made one party, to travel together as far as we could into the country of the Cheyennes. After that, they were to go on alone. They were mostly in the tail of the wagon train. They went down with a crash when the Pawnees charged. God help them!"

"Who went out commanding my father's men?"

"Your brother, sir."

"Jack?"

"Yes."

"Is he . . . hurt?"

"No, sir."

"Jack is commanding them," muttered Thunder Moon, turning the words over and over in his mind, with a total bewilderment.

"No man is keener to find gold than he is to find you, sir."

"Is that likely?" broke out Thunder Moon suddenly. Then he added: "Jack's come with the rest . . . to find me. It's got to be believed! Is there anyone else in the party that I know?"

"I think there are and particularly there is . . . ." Siegler checked himself.

"Go on, man."

"There is one you'd better see with your own eyes before you're told about, Mister Sutton."

Thunder Moon rubbed his chin with his hard

knuckles. He looked away across the prairie and he saw the men of his war party coming gradually back, some from such a great distance that they were mere specks. Others were disappearing in the hollows in part and growing big against the sky again, as they climbed the slight knolls.

It had been a great victory. The scattering drew back. In that sudden assault, not a single Cheyenne had been killed or seriously injured. Not a horse had been lost. Mortal fire having blazed suddenly in the faces of the Pawnees, they had fled without attempting more than a random and half accidental shot, here and there. A few grazes from bullets, a few shallow wounds caused by random lance thrusts or by knife cuts were all. Just enough had been done to raise the spirits of the warriors.

The pony-mounted volunteers from the village had not done such great execution upon their enemies, but even they had their scalps to show and their coups counted. Altogether seventeen Pawnees were dead and seventeen scalps were hanging from the bridles of the Cheyennes. There was not a man of the entire party who had not counted at least a single coup. It was a glorious victory. There was loot besides, in abundance, not only from the Pawnees but from the whites who had first been plundered by the Pawnees.

Young Snake, splashed with blood from head to foot —part of it running from a shallow, unregarded wound in his own broad right shoulder—came up to his leader with a face convulsed with joy.

"Take all the men and go back to the village," said Thunder Moon. "My band is tired. They have fought hard and ridden as only Cheyennes can ride. Go to Bald Eagle and ask him to send out some new men. The Pawnees are men. Spotted Bull is not among the dead,

48

and he may attempt to come back and fight once more."

"Spotted Bull," answered Young Snake, "is a brave man, for a Pawnee. But he has this day seen the fire of the Sky People flung in his face. He will not come again this day or this year within a week's ride of Thunder Moon and his men. I, Young Snake, saw him ride from the battle and never look back, but I shall do everything as you wish."

"Listen to me sharply," said Thunder Moon. "In the wagon train there are many white people who are my friends. They are to be treated as friends. They have come a great distance to find me. Let the young warriors come out and be a guard between the white men and the roaming Pawnees. Do you hear?"

"I hear and I shall tell Bald Eagle."

"Go to the teepee of White Crow, my foster mother. Give her the rifle and the clothes and all the weapons of this dead Pawnee. Load them upon his pony. Tell her that I killed him and two more with my own hand. She is an old woman and she needs to hear pleasant news to make her heart light and young again."

"Oh, my Father," said Young Snake—though Thunder Moon was much his junior, "it is no wonder that the Sky People love you. Your thought is always for others. This I shall do. White Crow shall sing louder than all the women of the Cheyennes. Also, they shall be silent while they hear her singing because of her son. Shall I go?"

"Go at once."

The other was off at once, gathering his men about him with shouts. Off went the warriors across the plain. There remained behind the dead, stripped bodies of the Pawnees, the whites, and Thunder Moon.

The whites gathered close around him, looking

49

fearfully across the plain, as though they expected terrible danger to flow in upon them from its vastness at any moment.

He reassured them gravely: "The Pawnees have lost heart. The Indians are not like the white men. When they are beaten, they go off to make new medicine. The white man stands up and fights again. Every kind follow their own ways. Tarawa sees it all. God, you call him, but he is one spirit."

Several horses had been left to them by the express command of Thunder Moon. The woman and the two children were mounted. The wounded Charles Siegler was slung in a rude litter between two ponies. So they started back across the prairie, Thunder Moon riding his great red stallion and leading the litter horses behind him.

The woman pressed eagerly forward. She was half weeping and half laughing. Her husband had been with her in the wagon which the Pawnees attacked. He had attempted to fight but, when the Indians surrounded him, he had tried to get through to the safe circle of the wagons before them. What had become of him she did not know.

She did not have to wait until they completed the entire journey to the wagon camp. A solitary rider loomed out of the grass before them, swept closer—and presently her high, tingling cry rang before her. The rider swept closer and embraced her. It was her man who had flung himself on a horse after the battle and determined to follow blindly on the trail of the Pawnees who had his wife and his child captive. Doubtless he would have died when the rear guard sighted him, but Providence had intervened on his behalf in the form of Thunder Moon and his band.

He came to that leader, when he had heard the story from his wife, and took the hand of the pseudo-Cheyenne in both of his. He could not speak. His face worked like the face of a child. Thunder Moon looked upon him with a strange happiness and sadness at once.

If he had not followed the first cruel working of his fancy, not a one of all the white men, his countrymen, would have fallen.

They journeyed on at a slow pace, controlled by the necessity of keeping to a gentle rate on account of the wounded man who, nevertheless, laughed at his own plight.

"They would have ridden us back to the Pawnee camp," he declared. "There the devil-women of the tribe would have buried splinters in me, and set 'em on fire. I know their little ways. May they all be damned!"

At last, far off, they saw the wagons, all exactly as Thunder Moon had seen them, the small, cramped circle at the head of the line and the rest of the wagons scattered in a broken line just as they had stood when the Pawnee charge broke into their midst.

He said to the happy husband: "John Sutton is in that train?"

"Him? Without him, we'd all be dead. He was drivin' the lead wagon . . . it was him that had the sense to turn in short and make the small circle . . . God bless him! He done a day's work that would've lasted him for the rest of his life." He added: "And the girl, too. I seen her handling her rifle like a man."

Thunder Moon asked no questions. An odd, stinging hope was awakening in his breast, and he looked with a scowl at the slow pace with which the litter bearers kept up the line.

In profound wonder he looked up to the broad surface

51

of the sky, now gathering color for the sunset time was upon them, and he saw one golden cloud high above the rest, with a bosom filled with rich fire. The Sky People! thought Thunder Moon. They have brought my brother out to find me.

CHAPTER NINE

"CAN I DO THAT?"

WHEN THEY CAME STILL CLOSER, THEY SAW THAT all the people of the caravan, more than a score, were gathered around a mound of newly turned earth—the common grave in which the dead had been placed. Thunder Moon could see afar the man who was reading the service for the burial. Three women were in the listening group—one of them had fallen to her knees in grief.

A little nearer, and now they could see faces. Yonder he knew the tall form of his handsome brother, Jack Sutton. Hardly a brother he had seemed in the old days. How different to find him here on the prairie.

A queer thrust of joy passed through the heart of Thunder Moon and his closed soul opened. He hurried on ahead of the others, scanning the group which had now turned away from the grave and toward him.

They began to shout. One of the women ran out with a wild cry that passed into the mind of Thunder Moon, never to leave him again.

She passed him and reached the litter and cried out again. There was as much agony of joy now in her voice as there had been agony of sorrow and pain and hope before.

Yonder man who had been reading from the Bible was now revealed as no less a person than Colonel Keene, looking no less courtly on the wide floor of the prairie than he had been in his own house.

Thunder Moon brushed straight on. His brother was hurrying toward him, calling out with honest joy in his voice—that same brother who once had so bitterly envied the man who had returned from the wilderness. Colonel Keene also moved forward, waving his hand in wonder and delight. Yet these people were hardly in the eye of Thunder Moon. He looked beyond them to the third woman—younger than the others, more slender— beautiful Charlotte Keene!

She did not advance with her father to greet Thunder Moon; rather she shrank back into the crowd. The more she shrank, the more savagely and well he knew that she loved him as much as ever he had loved her during the long and lonely months since he left her and rode westward toward the prairies.

The instant that he felt that hot wave of confidence in her, he could turn his attention to his brother and the colonel. They greeted him with the purest amazement, as well as joy. His hands were wrung. Big Jack Sutton danced like another Indian himself, and a thousand questions poured out.

How had he known that they were there? How had he chanced to come that way? He told them he had met Spotted Bull, trailed him, watched the attack on the wagons, sent in his challenge—which had the effect of drawing the cautious Pawnees hastily away from the rest of the wagons—intercepted him, sent back his men, and so here he was. After all, there was less of a miracle in this coincidence than had seemed, for had not the caravan been voyaging west these many weeks, striving

53

to find the section of the Cheyenne tribe to which Thunder Moon, alias William Sutton, was attached?

"Where's Charlotte?" asked the colonel. "She wouldn't let us go off without her when we started on this expedition. She wanted a taste of frontier life. God knows we've had too much of it today . . . the Pawnee devils."

Charlotte was with them at last, shaking hands and gravely telling William Sutton that she was glad they had found him. To Thunder Moon she looked almost childishly small, compared with the tall Cheyenne women. Even compared with Red Wind. All the other people of the tribe had to be met, and there was a glad hubbub of voices except from those who had lost friends or family in the battle.

To escape from that spot, Thunder Moon urged them to march straight on because they would find water within two miles. So the cattle, recaptured from the Pawnees, were put to the wagons, and the train forged ahead until the darkness came. Camp was made at the edge of a small stream. Men and animals drank. Three fires were lighted, for brush was plentiful. Dinner was cooked. All this while Thunder Moon had little opportunity for conversation because his presence was required here and there, directing the way, helping to picket the horses and oxen, and taking command in general.

Later he would have a chance to talk with Charlotte Keene. There was in him an infinite tide of things to say to her. When he came back to the fires after all of this work, he found that Charlotte had gone to the wagon to sleep. The other women and children, equally exhausted, disappeared under the canvas.

All the camp grew quiet. With low voices Colonel

Keene, Jack Sutton, and Thunder Moon talked together. They watched the head of the fire rise and snap off in the blackness, under the chin of the stars.

"One of you has done most of this," said Thunder Moon. "Which one is it?"

"We pulled together," answered the colonel gravely. "We did everything together. We each had our motives."

"And what was yours?" asked Thunder Moon of his brother.

Jack Sutton grew red, but his glance would not waver from the face of the other. "I had to find you," he said, "in order to let you know that I understood at last what an infernal puppy I'd been. I had to find you and tell you that I'd been a greedy fool . . . that I'd wanted to rob you of your rights . . . that I'd envied you the estate . . . great God, Will, I never could have called myself a man if I hadn't made some effort to find you. I'd even plotted against you . . . that last night . . . I'd betrayed you . . . or tried to . . . ."

Thunder Moon glanced at the colonel.

"He knows all about it," said Jack Sutton. "I told him and I told Charlotte. I'm clear with them at least. Perhaps some day I can be square with my own conscience."

"It was Harrison Traynor that put the killing into your mind," said Thunder Moon.

"It was," admitted the younger man.

Now across the firelight reached the great hand of Thunder Moon, so famous across the breadth of the prairies for its power. It was laid upon the shoulder of Jack Sutton.

"Brother," he said.

They looked full at one another with a world of

understanding and affection.

"We made up our minds to come after you. It was a long pull, we thought at the time. We joined with the caravan ten days ago. The length of the train was what nearly finished us off, as you had a chance to see. God knows that the rest of us were lucky to have you look on just then."

"Now that we've fairly met," said the colonel, "we must put the question which we've come to ask. Do you come back to your father's home with us?"

Thunder Moon frowned. Then he gathered the robe around his broad shoulders. He lighted his pipe and blew a puff toward the ground, and a puff into the air, and another cloud of smoke he struck with his hand and made it scatter into nothingness toward the horizon stars. In this Indian fashion he continued his smoking unconsciously, frowning in thought.

"I came back to my father's house," he said, "and I tried to live like a white man."

"A good job you made of it, almost from the first," said his brother.

"The first whites whom I saw hunted me like a fox. I settled down in the house and in the end, after a great deal of hard work with the brain and reading of books and sweating and grubbing and wearing stiff clothes that grip the shoulder muscles, in the end of all of this, when I had learned to love my father and mother and the old white house, I was driven away because I would not let my foster father lie in a jail."

"It was Traynor who did that," said the colonel. "God rest the dead, and Traynor is among them. I cannot help saying that I never heard of any more treacherous and devilish action than that of Traynor's against you, and the raising of the crowd to hunt you . . . when Traynor knew very well indeed that there were not three dead men left behind you in the jail. You'll find no more Traynors when you go back with us, my lad."

"There are other things," said Thunder Moon. "It is true that very often my heart is sick to go back among my own kind. Still here on the plains, a man is a man. There is freedom. There is no one to say to me: 'Go.' Or, 'Come.' Or, 'Stand.' "

"Who is there to say that to you in your own home, Will?" asked his brother.

"There are a good many things to stop me . . . pity for my mother . . . respect for my father . . . and always the hard fist of convention beating into a natural man's face . . . to say nothing of the law which keeps its rope around every neck."

The colonel at this smiled, and nodded. "Of course it's true," he said. "But, after all, there is something gained . . . polite conversation . . . culture . . . ."

"Have you ever listened to Indians telling stories?" asked Thunder Moon.

"No," admitted the colonel. He added: "With us, you would at once be a distinguished member of society. Your father is very old. Frankly, he is not very well. We don't expect him to live through the next winter. In case of his death, you would step up as the head of the family. The head of the whole estate."

"If I were head of the whole estate," said Thunder Moon, "could I then do as much as this?"

He whistled—a long, bird-like, mournful note—and then he raised a hand as a warning to listen. Almost at once, out of the darkness, they heard the rapid beating of the hoofs of a horse. Then into the firelight came a young Cheyenne. He brought the mustang to a halt close to the fire and raised long, slender lance and shield in salutation to Thunder Moon. That posture he maintained for a moment, unstirring, except as his lithe, muscular legs gave with the heaving ribs of the pony.

Thunder Moon spoke a few words in Cheyenne, and the warrior whirled the pony and was gone in a flash.

"Can I do that, when I am the head of the estate?" asked Thunder Moon.

CHAPTER TEN

FOR AND AGAINST

THAT WILD VISION OUT OF THE NIGHT WAS STILL IN THE minds of the listeners. They were still half dazzled by the wild light in the eyes of the mustang, in the eyes of the Cheyenne brave.

Then the colonel said slowly: "There are more than sixty slaves on your plantation, William."

"Here," replied the other, "I have more than twenty free men. If I go on the warpath, hundreds of others will follow me if I choose."

"To take scalps?" asked the colonel sharply.

Thunder Moon flushed. "I have never taken a scalp," he said.

"Come, come," said the colonel, "there is something to be said in favor of a comfortable house, contrasted with a shivering teepee in the winter snows."

"There is," admitted Thunder Moon, "but we have fire, food, and plenty of robes. The old men tell tales. There are always feasts, and the winters go away as fast as running water."

"That may be," replied the colonel, "but isn't it true, William, that you're held by something else more than anything that you've mentioned?"

"By what?"

"You have a pretty young wife among the Cheyennes, haven't you?"

"I?" exclaimed Thunder Moon.

"Let's be frank, my boy. The girl who speaks English. She herself told my girl that she was your wife."

"Red Wind?"

"Yes, that was her name."

"Said that she was my squaw?"

"That's right. What of it, William? That's not a disgrace. A man lives in Rome like the Romans. Besides, there are ways of arranging these matters. Only . . . I hope and trust that there are no children as yet William?"

"She told Charlotte that I am married to her?"

"No doubt she simply meant that she had been taken as a squaw, Indian fashion."

Thunder Moon set his jaw hard. "That explains a good many things," he said. "And your girl believed her!"

"I want to talk frankly," said the colonel. "You will imagine I had to have a pretty strong reason for making such a journey as this. A still stronger one for letting Charlotte go along with me. The fact is, William, that you were something more than a friend to her."

"I love her," said Thunder Moon quietly. "I told her so."

The colonel seemed to inhale this speech like incense. "If you care for her, that settles it," he said. "We'll arrange all of the minor difficulties. Then back you must come with us, my boy. Life has been a little drab and dark for poor Charlie since you left us."

"Suppose," said the pseudo-Cheyenne, "that I build a

59

trading fort in the hills. The Cheyennes would still be around us. Would Charlotte be happy here in the open country?"

"She has a thousand friends," said the colonel. "You know that, William. It would be hard to ask her to come out here. But I think she would do whatever you asked . . . except that you could not very well ask her to share your life with the Indian wife."

The colonel had put this as gently as he could, but his old eyes glimmered with ire and contempt as he spoke.

Thunder Moon arose.

"I go back to the village," he said, "and there I shall see Red Wind and bring her back with me to tell your daughter the truth. I have had no wife among the Cheyennes. Old White Crow, my foster mother, is the squaw in my teepee. I have placed a lodge for Red Wind near us. She was left alone in the world. I was a friend to her, and she has hurt me when my back was turned. But you will hear the truth from her own lips!"

The colonel fairly groaned with pleasure. "My dear boy," he said. "My dear lad! Bring her as fast as you can. Start with the morning. We'll head on in this direction."

"There will be Indians in front of you and around you," said Thunder Moon. "They are my friends, the Cheyennes, and they will keep you from trouble. Go to sleep now. You are all tired. In the morning I start for the village."

They took his word for it and went to their blankets, but Thunder Moon sat by the fire, the blanket huddled closely around his shoulders. He knew that he had come to a parting of the ways where he must choose one of the roads that branched before him. Drawing him toward the house of his father was his love of his family and the passion he felt for Charlotte Keene, and there was the pull also of his own blood and kind. On the other hand among the Cheyennes he was a force. He was like a king of the body and the spirit. There were other chiefs who led them, nominally, in war. But to Thunder Moon they turned as to a prophet and a preserver in times of evil. In peace they surrounded him with their adulation and their homage. He could not walk abroad without having respectful way made for him. The children flocked around him, as though to touch his hand would be to insure strength and fortune to them. Though he half knew that his mysterious authority was based upon a sham, yet in a way he could not be sure. The Sky People were to him half a superstition and half a fact.

The night grew colder and more still. The fires died. Only a blur of red light now glistened in the eyes of the picketed animals, or gleamed on the iron rims of the tires of the tall-wheeled wagons. This was the land of his knowledge and he loved it because he was familiar with it. Far away was the realm of the white man, and dreaded because it was unfamiliar.

Here upon the prairie he was a name which rang through all the red nations—Thunder Moon! But far to the east where his father's house stood, he was simply William Sutton, vaguely known as a man raised among the Indians—a nonentity—a thing without being, so far as the minds of other men were concerned. He sighed as he thought of it.

Looking up from his thoughts, he saw that it was the first glimmering of the gray dawn. Now he rose and, mounting the red stallion, he started back across the prairie. The Cheyennes swung in like gray ghosts to meet him, but he waved them back to their watch and bade them bring on the whites in the morning. Thus he went on swiftly.

The sun was half up over the horizon when the stallion waded through the creek and went up the slope beyond toward the village which already was up, for the Indian begins his day with the sun. Young women were coming down to the river for water. Boys stood about, shivering with the early cold. Warriors began to appear, wrapped in their buffalo robes. When he was sighted on his familiar horse, what a shout went up in welcome!

It was to Thunder Moon more than wine to the connoisseur. It was more than music to the music lover. Dignity was cast to the winds by these proud red men. They swarmed out about him. He had led them to battle the day before. The young braves had come back enriched in scalps, counting their coups. Half the night the scalp dance had lasted, the recounting of facts. Here was the author of that triumph.

They brought him in a tangle of cheers and exulting shouts to his lodge. He went in and found White Crow busily laying out the trophies which he had sent to her. It was rather a grisly sight. Complete in shirt and leggings of deerskin, heavily beaded because the dead man had been a Pawnee of note, with a mass of feathers for the headdress and with rifle and lance and knife and hatchet, it seemed as though more than a thin ghost of the dead were there.

White Crow turned to her foster son with a toothless grin of joy that almost made nose and chin touch.

"Last night a woman sang in the scalp dance," she said. "I told of the coups you had counted, oh, my son. I told how you had laid your braves in the tall grass. I told how the Pawnees were like puffs of smoke. You struck them and they disappeared forever. Spotted Bull is a great chief. He is a lucky warrior also. But my son is Thunder Moon. Ha! My soul is hungry to see the spirit of Big Hard Face. He must have leaned low from the happy hunting grounds last night to listen. All the people shouted your name together. Thunder Moon!"

He listened, delighted. If there was something childish about this, there also was something magnificent. He passed the pleasant thought away.

"Where is Red Wind?" he asked.

The jealous old squaw exclaimed: "Asleep, perhaps . . . that lazy creature. Or whispering with Standing Antelope. Hark what I have said to you a hundred times. No good ever has come from her. No good ever will come! She was bane to her father, bane to her people. She is poison and famine in the lodge. Now she talks with Standing Antelope. She makes his eyes as bright as the eyes of a hungry wolf. Is that a good thing? Be wise, Thunder Moon. A young woman is worse than firewater. Send her away. Give her to Standing Antelope. Let him have her!"

"Does he want her?" asked Thunder Moon gloomily.

"All the young men are fools. They look at her and turn their heads away as though she were a full sun in the middle of the sky. Do you ask me if they want her?"

"He is my friend," said Thunder Moon more cheerfully. "If he wants her, then he shall have her. First I must talk to her."

"Give her away . . . and talk to her afterwards," insisted White Crow. "She will not want to leave you. Now she has a lodge to herself. She only has to work for herself. Why should a useless woman wish to keep a lodge and do all the work for a warrior?"

Thunder Moon stepped outside the lodge and saw just before him a tall, athletic youth agape with pleasure and sorrow. Turning to look in the same direction, he saw Red Wind coming up from the river, carrying water, and the great braid of her copper hair shone like golden fire as it slipped down over her shoulder.

CHAPTER ELEVEN

HAPPY?

SHE CAME TO THUNDER MOON WITH A SMILE AND paused before him. He waved her on into her teepee and followed her in. She, putting down the skin of water, turned to him and offered him the place of honor on a folded robe, with a comfortable back-rest behind it. He refused with a curt gesture.

"Red Wind," he told her with a dignity of anger, "you have made me not happy."

She clasped her hands loosely before her and looked at him with submission.

"I am not wise," she said meekly. "Tarawa has not given me a mind like the sun or the moon. All of my days here seem to have gone by me like the wind over the prairie grass. Surely I have done nothing to make the great chief angry. I have had a dark thought, perhaps, and he has made medicine and he has read my mind."

Thunder Moon scowled darkly upon her. "Are you talking to some other person?" he asked. "Are you talking to some foolish other person, Red Wind? Between you and me there is an understanding. You know that the medicine I make is only for the eyes of the Cheyennes. We have no real belief in the Sky People."

"Do you deny them?" she asked him quickly. "Would

64

you stand under the open sky and tell them that you deny them?"

He sighed and shook his head. "There is no more strength in my mind than there is in a chain of grass," he admitted. "But that is not true of you. There is no foolishness in you, Red Wind. There is nothing in you except thought. You laugh at the Sky People and at all the Indian ways, and at all the Indian medicine. Tell me if that is true?"

"How should I say that," asked the girl quietly. "Who am I not to believe what my master believes?"

"I am not your master."

"What are you then?"

"I have only tried to be your friend."

"The lodge that I live in is yours," she said.

"I have given it to you," he answered.

"Gifts," she said, "are given to those who deserve them. What have I deserved from you? Nothing . . . nothing! I have brought you only trouble. But this lodge is yours, and the back-rests, and the weapons, and the beads . . . those bags and bags of them. Here out of the yellow and the green and the red beads, I have made you these moccasins, my master. I hoped to give them to you at a great feast but, now that you are angry with me, I give them to you as a peace offering."

She brought them to him. Made of the softest and the finest leather, she had worked them over with a consummate skill in strange patterns, such as he never before had seen. He took them and thanked her.

"But still you are laughing at me, Red Wind," he said. "In your heart you are laughing."

"In my heart, I am afraid."

"Why do you act as though you were a slave?" he said.

65

"What else am I?" she demanded. "I am not your daughter or your sister. If I were, you would sell me for a few horses to one of the men in the village. Perhaps you could find one who wants me. I am not your squaw. What am I, then, Thunder Moon?"

"Whenever you choose to play the child and be helpless," he grumbled, "there is no way that I can talk with you. But that is not fair to me, and I think that you know it."

"Tell me how I must speak to you," she asked. "The will of Thunder Moon is my will."

He stamped upon the floor of the teepee. "Do you want a husband?" he asked. "Twenty times I have begged you to tell me which one of the young men among the Cheyennes pleases you. Young Snake I have seen looking at you."

"What pleases you is pleasing to me," she replied.

"Answer me!" he commanded. "Tell me what you think!"

"Do I dare?" she asked plaintively. "Young Snake is a great friend of yours. He is your bravest warrior, next to Standing Antelope. If I should speak a bad word against him, you would beat me and have me weeping."

Thunder Moon went closer to her. He towered above her darkly.

"I have never raised a finger against any woman or against any child," he said. "This you know. Why do you speak to me in this fashion?"

Her eyes closed. "Oh, Thunder Moon," she murmured, "whatever I say is wrong. Whatever I do cannot please you."

"Speak truth, and be yourself," he begged. "There are wise women and cunning men among the Cheyennes, but there is none like you. I myself am only a child compared with you. Why do you act in this way? Is it because you are partly white and partly Indian?"

He eyes remained closed. He saw the long dark lashes against her skin. He could not tell why she had closed those eyes, or what thought was in her mind, or weariness, or disgust. From the beginning he never had been able to deal with her openly and easily. She was a problem beyond his solving.

"How can I tell what is the evil in me?" she asked. "Thunder Moon sees me, and understands much better."

He drew back from her, shaking his head. "Is it true that you hate me?" he asked her suddenly.

At this she opened her eyes. They were dull and angry.

"Hate?" she said.

"You saw the white woman whom I loved. You told her that you were my wife among the Cheyennes! That was a lie, Red Wind. Why did you lie to her?"

For almost the first time in his knowledge of her, he saw that she was staggered. Her color altered. She rested a hand against the nearest lodge pole.

"There are many rich men and wise men who loved her," said Red Wind at last. "Why should she have had you too?"

There was no acting now. Manifest fear was in her face.

He said slowly: "In spite of that, she has found me again."

"She!" cried Red Wind, starting most violently.

"She is one of the women in the wagon train the Pawnees raided."

"They could not find her body with a bullet!" cried the girl, with a sudden outbreak of savagery and despair.

Something like fear stirred the heart of Thunder

Moon. He looked at her in amazement.

"She is alive and well," he answered sternly. "You would gladly have seen her dead in the attack. Is that true?"

She did not answer but watched him with a sort of sullen defiance, as one who realized that she had said too much to retract.

"After this," went on Thunder Moon, "there is only thing you can do to help me. You must come with me to the white camp. You must go before her and tell her that on that other day you lied to her and that you never have been my squaw."

Red Wind turned pale indeed. "When must I go?" she asked.

"At once."

"Thunder Moon," said the girl in a trembling voice, "do what you wish to me today. But let me stay here till tomorrow in quiet. The wagon train will come close. It will be easier then for me to speak to her. I need a little time to think of what I must say. It is not easy even for a woman to admit that she has lied."

The big man sighed with pity. "That is true," he said. "Because of your pride, Red Wind, there are times when I admire you as I admire strong men. Because of beauty also, sometimes my heart has been open like the sky to the south wind, when it comes at the end of winter and turns the prairies green again. We shall wait until tomorrow before you speak to her. In the meantime it is not right that you should remain any longer as a part of my family. I see that bad talk has started. Everyone must be made to know that you are not my squaw, and it will be better for you to pick out a husband from among the Cheyennes."

She listened with great dark eyes that suddenly

narrowed in thought.

"Then I must choose a husband?" she asked.

"It is better. You see that. When you do not have me to take care of you, you must go into the teepee of some warrior of the tribe."

"Then let it be Standing Antelope, if he will have me."

"He is young," cautioned Thunder Moon.

"He is brave enough to ride at your side, Thunder Moon."

"Shall I send for him?"

"No. I shall ask a boy to go with a message to Standing Antelope. When he comes, then I shall talk with him and ask him if he would have me for a wife."

"There is little doubt of that!"

"I shall ask him how many horses he will pay you for me . . . how many would you demand, Thunder Moon?"

He flushed at this. "You think," he said, "that I have kept you in order to make myself richer by giving you to some chief for a wife? No, no! This lodge and everything in it is freely yours. All the beads, and the robes, and the dressed deerskins, and the knives and the saddles. Besides that, I shall give you one of my best horses . . . one of those tall red horses. Standing Antelope will be as rich as any man in the tribe when he takes you for a squaw."

She bowed her head. "My master is like one of the Sky People," she said. "Where he gives his kindness, he gives greatness and wealth also."

"You will be happy then, Red Wind?"

"Happy?" she exclaimed.

She threw up her head and broke into such a wild laughter that Thunder Moon backed out of the teepee with trouble in his heart and went slowly into his own lodge. There he found White Crow waiting for him, her brows quizzically raised and a smile of cruel satisfaction on her withered lips.

CHAPTER TWELVE

RED WIND'S VENGEANCE

LEFT NOW TO HERSELF, RED WIND SAW CLEARLY and calmly that her back was against the wall and she pushed back the grief and the rage which invaded her mind. There were two natures mingled in her—that of the white and that of the Indian. If she had the wild heart of an Indian, she had a white brain, calm and clear.

Since that old day when her father had brought her among these Cheyennes and palmed her off upon Thunder Moon, she had worked cleverly, insistently, in her own way to win the love of that hero of the ugly face and the wide shoulders. A dozen times she told herself that she was victorious but never with more certainty than when she had gone into the white man's land, to the very house of Thunder Moon, and there had managed to draw him away from the woman he loved. The triumph had seemed complete. She would have wagered her soul that before another moon passed she would be installed in the lodge of the hero. While many a moon came and went, she seemed as far from him as ever.

Now was the end. She knew it beyond doubt and beyond hope. He had learned of the artifice and the lie with which she had kept the white girl from him and there would be no forgiveness.

From the door of her lodge, she called a scampering

boy and asked him to carry her message to Standing Antelope. The boy was off like an arrow. It is a privilege to carry messages to a warrior so young, so brilliant, so famous. The girl retired once more into the lodge and sat down with her thoughts. The extent of her failure was clearer and clearer, and a boundless malice rose in her. All that love she had felt for the big man turned swiftly to poisonous grief, and then anger, and then settled hatred. She had offered him her soul in the palm of her hand, and he had turned his back upon her.

A voice at her lodge entrance. She called. Standing Antelope was before her. He was as different from Thunder Moon as were their names. The one was like a lordly bison bull, able to make the earth tremble and overawe the hearts of the strongest warriors. The other was like a soaring flame, as swift, as light, as dangerous. Those young hands of his had been filled with weapons by Thunder Moon himself, and by that warrior instructed in their use.

A painted buffalo robe was now gathered about the youth, but in spite of the things she could see that, like flame again, his whole body was trembling. His black, eager eyes gleamed at her. Here was fire, and it would burn at her bidding.

She stood up to greet him, gravely and gently, as she well knew how to speak to men, and she said in the metaphorical speech into which an Indian could always drop in time of need: "A woman should be like a child and never speak to warriors until she is first noticed. A shield which is cast down cannot leap up into the hands which own it, and a lance cannot strike if it has fallen to the ground and lies there unregarded. But I have been bold, and I have sent for you, Standing Antelope. White Crow will scold me for this. She will beat me

71

afterwards."

The warrior's hand made a convulsive movement. The robe parted and she saw that he instinctively had grasped the handle of a knife.

"The tongue of an old woman," he said, "is like the tail of a puppy. It cannot stop wagging. But there are ways to prevent the falling of blows, Red Wind."

"What could I do?" asked the girl, making her eyes large with helpless grief and fear. "What can all the Cheyennes do? Have they any strength to place against the strength of Thunder Moon?"

Standing Antelope jerked up his head and set his teeth hard. "There are more winds in the sky than one," he said darkly. "The rain does not come out of one cloud only."

She shook her head. "When Thunder Moon speaks, all the Cheyenne warriors tremble. When he lifts his hand, they all bow their heads. How should I dare to speak against White Crow, or stop her hand, if she raises an unstrung war bow to strike me?"

"To strike you!" said Standing Antelope, half choked with emotion.

She had slipped on the bank of the river and bruised her arm against a rock only the day before. Now, with a swift movement, she exposed her arm to the elbow and showed the discolored bruise.

"That was to keep the blow from my head," she said.

The young brave folded his arms across his breast, as though by the strength of his own hands he were striving to compress and control his excitement.

"There is a chief in this tribe," he said. "Bald Eagle is a chief."

"Shall I complain to him? He would laugh in my face and send me away, for fear lest Thunder Moon should

72

send disease to kill all his horses, or give him bad luck on the warpath."

Standing Antelope drew softly a step nearer: "You speak as people speak who do not know the whole truth. It is true that many of the warriors fear Thunder Moon. Many of them ride behind him. So do coyotes follow the grizzly bear, for the sake of the leavings after the kill has been made and the killer has feasted. The warriors are glad to ride behind Thunder Moon because, after he has struck, the least of the young boys are able to count coups and to take scalps. It does not mean that they follow him because they love him."

She looked down to the ground, to hide the burning exultation which she knew was springing up into her eyes. Then she sighed and said slowly: "If you give a horse grass from your hand, he is grateful and, if you throw meat to a dog, he kisses your hand. Therefore, of course the Cheyennes are grateful to Thunder Moon, and love him for the good he has done for them."

"They are not horses," said the youth, "and some of them are not dogs! Some of them know that Thunder Moon despises them. He uses them as men use a dog . . . to carry a burden, to run on an errand. He uses them at best like children. The council is called and all the old men speak, and the chiefs, and all of the experienced warriors who have taken scalps and counted many coups. After they have ended, Thunder Moon speaks like a voice from a cloud. He tells them that they have talked very wisely and very well, but he himself has wisdom from the Sky People and therefore they must do only what he advises them."

"But is it not true that the Sky People protect him and guide him?"

"Have you forgotten," said Standing Antelope, "how

73

he had to run for his life from the white people? They were his own kind and his own blood. But they kicked him out as one kicks out a mangy dog through the lodge entrance. If the Sky People work for him, why did Big Hard Face have to lay down his life to save that of Thunder Moon? Why did not Thunder Moon turn and take the lightnings out of the sky and throw them in a river of fire against his enemies? No, we have seen him hunted with horses and dogs and guns, like a wolf. We have seen him running. Therefore, I say that all his talk about the Sky People is a great lie."

Having said this, Standing Antelope turned suddenly a little more toward the entrance, and his body stiffened. His glance rolled anxiously upward, as though he half expected that, in reward for such a blasphemy, the thunders of the actual sky might at that moment descend upon his head.

The girl saw and a faint smile of understanding and contempt flashed upon her lips, glimmered in her cold eyes, and was gone again. This boy was a tool, and no more than a tool. With him she could strike a glorious blow of revenge, she felt. She summoned an expression of terror and wonder and ran to the youth.

"Standing Antelope," she whispered. "Beware! Pray quickly to Tarawa before you are stricken. Pray for protection."

His lips were pale purple with his fear, but presently he mastered himself again and said as stoutly as he could: "You see that nothing happens. I am safe. I am safe because I am not afraid of Thunder Moon."

She affected an air of intensest admiration: "Oh, Standing Antelope," she said. "Is it true then? Are you alone among the Cheyennes able to stand against Thunder Moon? Are you alone able to save me from

74

him?"

"Are you in danger from him?" asked the brave. "Does *he* also strike you?"

"The heaviest blows are not given with the hand," she said.

He waited, keen as a knife, for more.

"See how he keeps me here," she said. "I am neither his slave nor his sister nor his squaw. I am nothing! I am like a dog on a chain. It can only be seen. So am I. Thunder Moon keeps me here. He keeps me here so that he can point me out to strangers and to the whole tribe. It is because I satisfy his pride. He shows them what I am. 'She is not worthy to be my squaw' is what he means to say to them."

Standing Antelope made a gesture in the sign language. For many a time the Indian, overcome with emotion, still will speak in the language of gesture which is known to the entire people of the plains. Unable to speak, he now expressed vast wonder that what he heard should be true. She continued in haste, following up the effect which already had shocked him so: "What life have I? Even a horse is at least allowed to walk out to the pastures and run with the wind. But I cannot do that. If he will not have me, why will he not let others have me? What am I to him that he should want to keep me here? If a warrior or a young brave so much as looks at me, Thunder Moon frowns terribly, and the warriors turn their heads away and pretend that they were not looking at me at all."

She allowed her voice to rise softly to a little breaking point of vexation and grief.

Then Standing Antelope, his voice as shaken now as his body had been before, exclaimed: "This is wonderful, Red Wind! We all have thought . . . all of the warriors and the young braves . . . that you cared for nothing except Thunder Moon. That you lived because he willed you to live, and breathe because he willed you to breathe. Have we all been wrong?"

"Look at his picture in your own mind!" she answered with a wild enthusiasm of anger, letting her hatred shine boldly from her eyes: "Is there an uglier face on all of the prairies?"

CHAPTER THIRTEEN

THE DOUBLE EDGE

PERSONAL BEAUTY DID NOT, AS A RULE, GREATLY disturb the thoughts of young Indian girls. Instead, they were more apt to fill their minds with the number of horses their prospective husband might own, the quantity of beads or weapons in his possession. A fine headdress of nodding feathers was apt to be more to them than the features of an Apollo.

Standing Antelope looked deeply into his mind and did not see any corresponding image for a moment. Then he stared at Red Wind again. Even among the white women of Thunder Moon's true people, he had remembered no beauty like hers. Next he recalled the heavy brow and the great aquiline nose and the broad jaw of Thunder Moon.

For his own part, he always had admired those features and envied them for fierceness and strength. That face, with battle shining in the eyes, had more than once made Blackfoot and Pawnees and Sioux flinch from the charge. He could see that the girl might have another viewpoint.

Beauty then for the beautiful! As he thought of this, he could not help but remember his own image in polished metal, in the mirrors which had amazed him in the house of Thunder Moon's father, and in the standing water of a pool when he leaned to drink. A shock of hope and pleasure ran hotly through the veins of the young brave.

"Tell me then," he said suddenly, "you always have hated Thunder Moon?"

"Ah, Standing Antelope," she said, "you have drawn the truth out of my heart. I could conceal nothing from you. Now you will go to Thunder Moon. He will kill me for speaking as I have spoken."

The warrior answered with a strange quickness.

"What you have told me is as much a secret as though you had spoken it only to your own heart. Will you believe that?"

"If you have said it. There are no lies on your tongue, Standing Antelope. All the other Cheyennes might scorn a woman so much they would not tell her the truth. They laugh in my face perhaps. But you are too proud to lie even to a woman."

He said: "You want freedom, Red Wind?"

"Ah, yes! I die for the lack of it, friend."

"I have not," said the youth, "a herd of great horses like Thunder Moon. I have not many rifles. I am not followed by many braves. Yet if you will come with me, as I tried to say to you not many days ago . . . ."

"Would you take me?"

"I? Tarawa see my heart."

"In spite of all the Cheyennes? Thunder Moon would follow us."

"The prairie is broad."

"The Sky People would point out our trail to him."

"Listen to me," said the boy, "I have often been with him on the trail and, once away from the camp, Thunder Moon is glad to let the other braves lead. He will not ride out from the camp unless he has in his party a good trailer, one who knows by a glance at the trampled grass how long before a horse had stepped upon it. No matter how the Sky People befriend him, they leave him blind upon the plains. This I know. I, as a young man, have shown that great chief the way, like a child led through the darkness."

"If he started to pursue us, he will have the finest trailers in the tribe to ride with him."

"Perhaps he will not pursue. There is a certain bigness in his heart. He might not pursue. He might simply let us ride away. I do not think that he would beg a woman to return to him after she once wanted to go away."

"Then why has he kept me here, like a wretched slave?"

He was silent, brooding upon this point. Remembering in a flood his old affection for Thunder Moon and all of the courage and the strength and the kindness which he had found in that famous man, his heart failed him a little. He looked at the girl with a keen thrust of suspicion.

She met that glance with a steady boldness of eye. He sighed. Her beauty was a solvent which loosened all of his thoughts. He could not face her and remain true to himself and the better heart which was in him.

"If we fled away together," said the girl, "he would not long remain behind us. He would soon pursue with others."

"Let them find our trail. We shall outride them if we cannot outwit them!"

"Who can outride the red horses?"

He struck his hands together.

"It is true," he admitted in despair. "It is very true that no one could ride away from the twenty men on his great horses." Then he added: "You are wise. Even Thunder Moon has asked for your advice and followed your counsel. Be wise now, Red Wind, and tell me what I can do. Look at me only as two hands which are willing to work for you."

It was exactly the point to which she had wished to bring him, but now she affected sorrow and despair in her turn again.

"There is only one way," she said.

"By which we could escape from him?"

"Yes."

"Then let me know."

She shook her head.

"You beg for your freedom. You will not open the door to it!" he exclaimed eagerly.

"It would be my freedom and your death," she said.

Sobered a little, he stared at her. With the slender staff which he carried in his hand, he struck upon the hard-packed earthen floor of the lodge.

"Who can tell when death will come?" he said. "I have done something in my life. I have counted coups. I have taken scalps. I have made myself known among the Cheyennes. The enemies of my people have heard my name. The chiefs come to me and speak kindly. When a party goes out upon the warpath, they ask me if I shall ride with them. I, like a fool, have refused to go, except when Thunder Moon was my leader. I have done something and, now, why should I be afraid to die? I am not afraid. Tell me in what way we can go free then?"

"I am his captive," she said slowly, "as long as he lives. But a dead man has no hands to hold even a weak woman."

At this sudden suggestion, no matter how she had tried to lead up to it, the warrior shrank a little, and looked at her as though she had opened a pit that looked down to the bottom of the world.

He said at last, rather huskily: "To murder Thunder Moon?"

She did not answer. Passion, vengeance, envy, jealousy, dead love were all in her face. But no matter what feeds the fire, it casts a light. So her beauty, half Indian and half that of a white woman, flared before the eyes of Standing Antelope, and puzzled and bewildered him.

"Do you know," he said, "what comes to the man who murders in his own tribe?"

"He is outcast forever."

"That is true," said Standing Antelope. "I should be a man without a people."

"But Thunder Moon is no Cheyenne!"

"He is more than that. He is a stranger who has been trained among us. He has left us, and still he has come back. At this moment the warriors are speaking of him. His name is filling up their mouths since he drove Spotted Bull like a dog across the prairies."

"Let that be true," she said. "Ah, Standing Antelope, you do not know me. My heart has been full for many years. I have had no way to give out what is in it. If you were with me, I think that I could make you happy, even as a man without a people."

He did not touch her. A dazed look came in his eyes merely.

"It is time," said Standing Antelope simply. "When shall I kill him?"

"This night, this night!" said the girl with a wild

eagerness. "Kill him this night, and then we shall ride under the cover of the darkness."

Amazed, he stared at her.

"Will you love as you hate?" he asked her.

"You will see," said the girl. "There is no flesh in me. There is nothing but fire, Standing Antelope. Kill this man, and then we may be happy together. If he lives, I shall burn up like a leaf in the autumn sun."

He hesitated, his eyes wandering swiftly from side to side.

"The best of all that is in the lodge I shall pack," she assured him.

She had mistaken his meaning. He answered hotly: "This was the gift of Thunder Moon. There is nothing here that is really yours. Take nothing. Strip off your rich clothes and the beadwork. If you have some old, tattered dress, take that."

"At least, we shall ride off on two of the red horses."

"Not for a single stride!"

"But he has given two of them to you."

"They are his gift," said the other sullenly and sadly. "I want nothing that is his. I shall not take the rifles he has given to me. Look. Nearly everything that I have is his gift. But I shall throw everything away except the little that is my own. I wish that Tarawa would give to me the power to strip off from my mind the things which Thunder Moon has taught me. That I cannot do. But if he has made my hand skillful, he has only given it the skill which will take his own life."

At this, as though the saying of the word brought up the vision of the dead brightly before him, he straightened himself with a swelling breast before her. And great, desperate eyes. Then he turned, and went hastily out of the lodge without speaking another word.

She, following to the flap of the teepee, looked after him and saw him going off with a rapid but uncertain step. She gripped her right hand hard. Standing Antelope was a keen knife, to be sure, but the metal was apt to snap under a strain, she felt.

CHAPTER FOURTEEN

BROTHERS

IN THE HEART OF THE AFTERNOON, THE WAGON train came up. It did not cross the river, but remained upon the farther side of it, at the express suggestion of Thunder Moon. He too often had seen that white men and red cannot agree very long together, and the first gladness of meeting rapidly turns to trouble. He decided that he would keep the current of the river between the two camps.

Almost immediately, however, there was a flood of the red men among the wagons, their eyes and then their hands prying everywhere. Thunder Moon stood in the center of the camp and raised his great voice. Great as thunder it boomed and rolled among the scattered wagons of the circle. When he had finished his brief admonition in the Cheyenne tongue, the Indians gathered together and slunk off toward the river. Only their chiefs remained.

Bald Eagle had come bearing a present of beaded moccasins and three Indian ponies, the fattest and therefore the best of his herd.

Colonel Keene received him, with Thunder Moon acting as the interpreter, received the presents, made others in return, chiefly of good knives of which the tribe at this moment was in great need. For working on hides of tough buffalo bulls and cows for teepees wears out knives faster than anything in the world.

The exchanges being made, the colonel showed himself astonishingly liberal to other chiefs who had accompanied Bald Eagle, until that dignitary, his arms literally filled with what to him were magnificent treasures—strings of beads hanging from his arms and half a dozen hickory hafts for axes thrusting out like pins from a pin cushion—at last said to Colonel Keene:

"In the land of the white man, there is a great medicine. It turns thoughts into knives and bullets, and wishes into beads and bright cloth. We only can give you meat and robes of buffalo hides. But our hearts are very warm. We thank you and we thank Thunder Moon who has drawn so many good things to the Cheyennes."

The chiefs departed. Colonel Keene set about looking for William Sutton in person, but that unreclaimed white man was seated in a corner of the wagon circle lost in conversation with Charlotte Keene. The colonel, after one long look, turned elsewhere.

Thunder Moon had said to the girl: "The Cheyennes do not tell lies except to public enemies. I am going to call the biggest of the chiefs. You shall hear him say whether or not I have a wife among his people."

But she answered frankly: "Do you think that I've come all these hundreds and hundreds of miles to argue with you, or to take testimony? I don't care! There's only one important thing . . . which is that you and I are sitting on the double trees of this particular wagon in this particular place. I know that and I don't care about the rest."

He watched her with a content too deep for speech. All that existed on the prairies seemed, at that moment, little enough compared with her.

"If you've come here," he said suddenly, "would you stay here, Charlotte?"

She looked down to the ground. He could feel that she had been struck a blow, but she glanced up to him again almost immediately, and said: "I can stay here."

"It would be a wilder and a harder life than you've been accustomed to," he assured her.

"Not so hard as my life since you left me, William."

He was silent for a moment, listening to an echo of her voice, as it were, pronouncing his Christian name— so long unfamiliar in his ears.

"I could build a house for us. Do you see where the hills begin to go up there?"

"It looks like blue, rolling smoke."

"Yes."

"I see them more clearly now."

He smiled at her.

"You will learn to use your eyes in this country. If you look still harder, you'll see the mountains beyond the hills."

"They're almost lost against the sky," she said.

"The fleck of white . . . more blue than white, but with a shine in them . . . those are the snow caps of the mountains."

"Ah!"

"There where the hills and the mountains divide?"

"Yes, I see the gap, I think."

"A great river comes down from the highlands there. I've chosen the valley. We could build there."

"Yes," she said.

"Does the thought of it make you sad?"

"Nothing really makes me sad today," she answered obliquely.

This humility in her disturbed him more than any prayers that he should go back with her to the whites of her home. He remembered her in other days, imperially ruling among the youth of the countryside and the old white houses. Now she submitted, swallowed all argument.

He, watching her more closely, saw the stain of blue beneath her eyes which made them seem larger and deeper. Grief had placed that stain there, he knew well enough. A great tenderness came upon Thunder Moon. He scanned her more and more closely, like a book—a book whose mere title he had seen and loved before, but this was all the closely compacted print, filled with infinite meaning he had not known. Her very face was half strange to him. The longer he gazed, the more deeply he was staring.

"You think of your friends," he said.

"Yes, I think of them."

"If you think of them a little today, you will think of them a great deal later on."

"Perhaps. But that will not keep me away, William. I'm not a weak thing, to sit and mourn and complain. You must trust me in saying that."

"I *do* trust you. Out of this thing we're going to find happiness, Charlotte."

She turned her head and smiled at him and, by that single glance, he knew truly the depth of her love which had brought her here to him. Facts could not have demonstrated it, any more than words can illustrate music.

He went to the colonel and told him the conclusion briefly. "Charlotte agrees that she'll try to live out here with me."

The colonel sighed. "Charlotte would agree to

anything," he said. Then he added: "Now, my lad, I won't begin with giving you advice. Your lives are your own. Only permit me to say: no one gets something for nothing in this world of ours. We pay as we go. A bad investment leaves you bankrupt in the end."

"I don't quite understand that."

"I mean that the sorrow you cause is the sorrow that you will eventually have to feel."

Thunder Moon, turning this thought in his head, went back toward the village. There was to be a feast at which all the chief men would appear. The colonel and Jack Sutton would be there.

Indeed, he found Jack Sutton already in the village, having broken through the express orders that no one was to leave the wagon circle. Jack was surrounded by a large and curious throng. Men and women pressed about him. Children dived reckless among the edge of their elders, and so strove to creep through the forest and come to the sight of the white man. As Thunder Moon came up, he heard over and over again the simple phrase:

"It is the brother of Thunder Moon! It is the blood brother! It is the brother of our medicine man!"

He smiled a little, with a lifted heart. Standing Antelope at that moment went by hastily, with his light, noiseless step, and Thunder Moon reached out to him and caught him by the shoulder.

The boy winced away from the grip and turned for an instant a dangerously darkened face. Every Indian is the master of some degree of dissimulation and, almost instantly, he made his face clear again.

"You still are a sick man," said Thunder Moon gently. "I shall have to take care of you. You must come to my lodge and eat what White Crow cooks for you.

She is a wise old woman. She knows the herbs."

"My brother is kind," said the youth, his voice extraordinarily faint.

"Look," said the big man, "you are pale. Your very voice is weak. You no longer are always dancing on the tips of your toes, trying to make yourself taller. Ha? Standing Antelope, I shall have to pay more attention to you. If you had been with me yesterday, you would have taken three scalps and counted half a dozen coups, and that without the slightest danger. I must have you closer beside me from this time forward."

Standing Antelope said not a word.

"Have you seen my brother Jack?"

"No."

"What? Not seen him yet? See how they crowd around him. But we'll break through, I think."

He laughed with pleasure at the thought of his power over these wild people. Jack Sutton was calling: "They have me half choked with dust already, Will!"

At a single word from Thunder Moon, the crowd opened and gave back rapidly. They smiled and chattered gaily at the sight of the two brothers, standing side by side, and exclaimed hastily: "But he is not so tall! Nor so wide! Nor so big in the feet and the hands! He is hardly a brother to Thunder Moon!"

Thunder Moon strode on, dragging Standing Antelope with him, and exclaimed at last: "Here's my brother among the Cheyennes, Jack! You've not forgotten Standing Antelope?"

Standing Antelope, who understood the words perfectly, closed his teeth hard to keep back a groan.

CHAPTER FIFTEEN

WITH STEEL IN THEIR HANDS

IT WAS BALD EAGLE IN PERSON WHO NOTED THE wild and unhappy look of Standing Antelope and took occasion to stop him a little apart from the crowd.

"Brother," said the war chief, "your friend has become greater than ever on this day. Therefore, you are greater also, and yet I see a shadow on your forehead. How can this be?"

The boy answered nothing for a moment but considered the older man. At length he said grimly: "Your arms have been filled with presents. Another such a day and you will have to live in two lodges. One for yourself and one for your wealth. Still you do not seem happy, Bald Eagle."

That battered chieftain frowned at this readiness of tongue in so young a warrior, and he said sternly: "A youth listens. An older man speaks!"

"To what do *you* listen, then?" asked Standing Antelope. "To your own heart, do you not?"

"All men listen to their voice of the spirit," said the chieftain.

"Let me tell you, then," said the boy, "that your heart has been beating so loudly that even I heard it."

Bald Eagle could not make a reply, but it was plain that he was startled.

"I have heard your heart say," went on Standing Antelope, "that although your arms have been filled with gifts...beads and guns and powder and lead and knives...and everything that the heart of a great warrior could wish, yet you had rather that this day and those

88

presents never had come to you."

The chieftain pulled his robe about his shoulders with a convulsively impatient gesture.

"What do you wish to say to me, Standing Antelope?" he asked. "Have you been drinking the white man's firewater and grown dim in the brain, like a mountain wrapped in a mist?"

"I have not been drinking firewater," said the boy, "but I have been looking at the heart of the great chief and war leader, Bald Eagle, and I see fire in it . . . smoke and fire about to break out. The heart of Bald Eagle is very hot. Of what use is his name as war chief? The young men follow Thunder Moon on the warpath. How do they regard Bald Eagle? He is only a name and no more to them."

The chief was thrown into such a frenzy of anger by this speech that, for a moment, he seemed about to fling himself at the throat of the youngster, but he controlled himself long enough to say in a voice like distant thunder: "Has he sent you to me to give me these taunts?"

Standing Antelope answered quickly: "Look at me, Bald Eagle! It is not as a stranger or a spy that I have understood what is within you."

Bald Eagle's wrath was quite dissipated by astonishment as he listened to this speech, and he answered: "Young man, do I understand that you are telling me that Thunder Moon no longer is your friend?"

"How can he be my friend?" answered the boy. "He keeps in a lodge beside him a woman, like a dog on a chain. He would not give her to me for the price of a hundred good horses."

"Red Wind...Red Wind!" exclaimed the chief softly. "I know that friendship is more powerful than rawhide

89

ropes, well twisted. But a woman is stronger still. With a touch of her hand she snaps stronger ropes of kindness than these. The Sioux give us war outside the camp. Our women give us battles inside our lodges. That is what has happened to you, Standing Antelope."

The boy, somewhat heated by the implied reproach or contempt in the words of the other, said hastily: "When a man is sick of a great fever, does he laugh at the doctor who can cure him?"

Bald Eagle's eyes narrowed to squints.

"One says to the doctor, how will the cure be made? With prayer and medicine . . . or how?"

Standing Antelope looked swiftly about him, and then stepped closer.

"With the knife," he whispered.

The nostrils of Bald Eagle expanded.

"Come with me," he said. "It is plain that we have much to say to one another."

Never in the history of the tribe had there been a greater feast. An Indian feast is not made with food but with conversation and here, present among them, were the kin of that man of mystery, Thunder Moon. They looked at the thoughtful face of the colonel, and upon the handsome, pale features of Jack Sutton. They said among themselves: "Truly, Thunder Moon has something more than an Indian name and a Cheyenne tongue. He has also no little part of the blood of a Cheyenne by sympathy. See his face! It is almost as dark as ours! His features are those of an Indian. His hair and his eyes are as dark as ours. His way is our way and he is one of us!"

While Jack Sutton was saying to his brother: "You are a great man to these people, Will."

"Do you wonder," said Thunder Moon, "that I can't leave them forever?"

"You could come out to see them every year or so," suggested Jack Sutton.

"Perhaps I could. But the tribe would be wandering. They might be scattered to the four winds before I came back again. As a matter of fact, I think that I have had some share in holding them together."

"They admire you. They know that you're useful," said Jack Sutton, "but how many friends have you really among them?"

"There is Standing Antelope," answered the big man. "He's young, but he's a man. I've seen him tested in fire."

"Where is he tonight?"

"Sick, in his lodge. I've been to see him. He has a fever. Hands dry and forehead hot. Tomorrow I begin a course of medicine for him."

"He has a dark look, that youngster," said Jack Sutton. "Who is that about to speak?"

"They are passing the coup stick," said Thunder Moon, smiling faintly. "Do you hear?"

"I hear, but I don't understand. What does the hard-faced old chap say?"

"That he who has counted five and thirty coups in battle shall be permitted to hold the stick and count three coups which he has struck. This is a compliment to me, Jack. You see, none of the rest has counted so many.

"I shall count one coup," the narrator said in Cheyenne. "The Comanches sleep in a great tent. The Yellow Man is among them, a great medicine. Among all the Comanches there is no medicine half so strong as this."

A murmur went through the circle. A hundred times they had heard the story, and a hundred times their eyes had gleamed exactly as they gleamed now.

"The circles of the warriors sleep with bows and rifles at their sides," continued the narrator. "But one man comes among them. He is a Cheyenne. He goes from tent to tent like a shadow. The Sky People breathe in the faces of the sleepers. They are like the dead. The stranger passes . . . one man rises, half awake. The Cheyenne strikes, and the man is still. His medicine bag is in the hands of the Cheyenne. His soul is lost forever. The warrior goes on. His heart is not afraid. He comes to a greater tent. It is the medicine lodge. Within it sleeps one man, or hardly sleeps. He rises. He prays. He prays to the Yellow Man. The shadow of Thunder Moon soon falls upon him. He feels the cold hand of death. The hand reaches forth and is laid upon him. He is dead. The Yellow Man is taken. Upon him Thunder Moon counted a great coup! He struck the face of the Comanche medicine. He waited, ready for thunder and lightning. But nothing followed. The Yellow Man did not stir. Thunder Moon picked him up and fled with him through the camp. He was followed, but he escaped. Comanches lay dead behind him. There was blood on his hands. He came again to his friends. The Comanches had lost their strong medicine. This coup that I counted was a true coup. It was struck on the body of the Yellow Man."

He passed the coup stick from him.

"Let he who has counted fifteen coups receive this stick!"

Thunder Moon translated to his brother softly, and added: "Bald Eagle can speak of this coup. He's a great warrior."

Bald Eagle spoke. Others followed. Briefly, and in murmurs, Thunder Moon translated the sum of the tales which were narrated, and the other two white men beside him listened, fascinated, to bloody and wild deeds done in the midst of fierce battles, or in the camp of the enemy in the dead of the night.

The night grew old. The colonel himself was asked to narrate one deed he had done. He told, briefly—while Thunder Moon translated—of an adventure with Gulf pirates while on a pleasure cruise—and Jack Sutton contributed a narrative of the hunting of the marsh brigands through their lairs. There was much applause and, at length, with a prodigious handshaking all around, the feast ended. Thunder Moon accompanied his brother and the colonel out of the tent.

A crowd followed but left them at the edge of the village.

"As odd and interesting an evening as I ever passed through," said the colonel. "But why are you downhearted, Thunder Moon?"

"Because," said the other, "I cannot understand this. They should have sent out twenty young men . . . with torches, perhaps . . . to show us the way to the wagons. I don't understand it. What's in the mind of Bald Eagle?"

"He's forgotten, of course."

"Indians never forget their manners until they are about to run amok," replied Thunder Moon and, still gloomily thoughtful, he went with the others down the slope toward the bank of the river.

"I go first," he said. "Watch the rocks that I step on. At this height of the water, there's no need for you so much as to wet the soles of your boots. Watch me cross, and then follow."

He went lightly, jumping from rock to rock, across the river. As he reached the farther shore and turned toward his two companions who were about to follow, silent, shadowy forms arose from the brush behind him, with the gleam of steel in their hands.

CHAPTER SIXTEEN

ON THE RIVER

THE QUICK OLD EYE OF THE COLONEL SAW THE DANGER first. His shout of horror was not a word— simply a vague, piercing cry—and it turned Thunder Moon about to find bright-edged steel gleaming in his very eyes and the voice of Standing Antelope exclaiming: "No bullets! No bullets! Bullets never can kill him! Only the edge of the knife! Only the edge of the knife!"

But if bullets could not kill Thunder Moon, knives surely were at his throat. He leaped far back from the rush, his revolver coming into his hand as he sprang, and he made out, with horror and bewilderment, that one of those close assailants was no less a person than that trusted lieutenant, Young Snake. Two more came behind the first pair, with Standing Antelope rushing into the lead, swift as a panther.

A gun boomed heavily from across the river. It was Jack Sutton's rifle, for he had carried the gun with him and, with a shot which was partly quick skill and partly luck, he set a bullet through the head of Thunder Moon's right hand man. The fellow toppled without a sound, his loose shoulder striking literally across Thunder Moon's knees. A shot from the Colt doubled up the second of the leaders, and there was Standing

94

Antelope, coming in with the screech of a wildcat. There was time for a bullet, but in the last instant Thunder Moon could not draw the trigger. Instead, he swayed aside from the flash of steel, and struck at the lithe body with his fist. Hard upon the ribs the blow struck home. Standing Antelope, stunned, bruised, breathless, dropped writhing upon the river bank.

The fourth man had swerved like a football player as he saw the mischief into which his companions had fallen and was merely a crackle of faint sound as he shot off through the brush.

Thunder Moon did not follow. Heartsick and bewildered, he leaned over the fallen. Young Snake was gasping out his last breath. Over him Thunder Moon leaned as his brother and the colonel came floundering through the water to get to his side, quite missing the way across the dry rocks.

As he leaned over Young Snake, Thunder Moon saw plain recognition and plain hatred in the face of the wounded brave.

"Young Snake," he said, "I have mounted you with one of my best horses. I have led you on to much honor. Never before had you counted a coup or taken a scalp until you came among my followers. Why have you tried to murder me like a wolf of a Pawnee?"

"Because I am not your dog, to come and go when you whistle. And because . . . I hated your pale face."

So spoke Young Snake, and snapped at the air over his shoulder with a last convulsion of savagery and fury, and died.

Thunder Moon leaned above Standing Antelope, who was raising himself to his hands and knees. He stood upright and folded his hands across his breast. He was naked to the waist. He was painted as for war. Two eagle feathers were thrust into the long black masses of his hair, which glimmered in the starlight. He waited in silence for the falling of the blow as the colonel and Jack Sutton came breathlessly ashore.

"Standing Antelope!" cried Jack in horror.

Thunder Moon waved the two aside and drew the boy aside.

"I am sick with sorrow and trouble," said Thunder Moon bitterly. "You too, like Young Snake, always have hated me?"

The boy tried to answer, and at length he forced from his lips a gasping: "The Sky People still watch over you. Strike me now to the heart. I shall not speak again."

"Lad," answered the older man gently, "we have traveled too many trails together. You are as free as though you still were my best of friends among the Cheyennes. Tarawa forgive you and purify your mind. Will you not tell me what made you come at me . . . in the night . . . with three fighters to help you? Murder, Standing Antelope! Thank the spirits who have saved you from it!"

Standing Antelope, trembling like a leaf, answered: "I did not hate you always, as the rest have done. It was because you would not take Red Wind for yourself, nor give her to anyone else."

Thunder Moon exclaimed in bewilderment: "This very day I told her that she should take you for a husband. This very day, Standing Antelope! Are you mad?"

"You?" cried the boy. "You told her that?"

"Yes, yes. This morning. When I came to speak to her, because she had said among the whites a thing about me that was not true."

"Ha!" breathed Standing Antelope, and reeled

96

heavily.

The arm of Thunder Moon supported him. "My young brother," he said, "she has lied to you also. Is it truth?"

"Why?" groaned Standing Antelope. "What devils could be in her?"

"I shall find her for you, if you want her, and give her to you, for that is my right," said Thunder Moon.

"Shall I make a lie into my squaw who keeps my lodge and raises my children?" asked the boy fiercely. "But now I see more things, and more clearly. It is the white squaw, oh, Thunder Moon! It is the white squaw that has driven Red Wind mad with jealousy. On account of her she has tried to bring about your murder and she has simply used my knife! She said that she would wait for me up the river at the three trees. But now I know that she will not be there. She has betrayed you. She has betrayed me. Why was I ever born?"

He turned from Thunder Moon and ran off through the brush, heading swiftly up the river.

Thunder Moon turned back to his two white companions. Down from the village, on the farther side of the river, came dancing lights, as men and boys ran to learn what had caused the wild shouts and the explosions of guns. The light of the torches fell like the tresses of gleaming red hair, spread over the surface of the water.

"See," said the big man slowly. "The river was between me and my life as a Cheyenne. The river is between us, and I never can cross it again. There is blood upon the water. This night my friends have gone from me. I was a Cheyenne. My name was Thunder Moon. All the prairies knew me. But Thunder Moon is dead. Do you hear? The knife of Standing Antelope found the heart of that chief. He is dead. He will return no more."

He started resolutely ahead, drawing the two with him.

"I was two people in one," he said, with a sudden calmness, "but now one half of me is dead. I am going home to my own people. I am William Sutton at last."

Farther up the river the Cheyenne boy, Standing Antelope, leaped breathlessly out from the covert and ran beneath the three trees where Red Wind should have been waiting for him.

She was not there. There was no sight of her. There was no sound. Only the wind hushed through the leaves of the trees with a hissing sound.

ABOUT THE AUTHOR

MAX BRAND™ is the best-known pen name of Frederick Faust, creator of Dr. Kildare, Destry, and many other fictional characters popular with readers and viewers worldwide. Faust wrote for a variety of audiences in many genres. His enormous output, totaling approximately thirty million words or the equivalent of 530 ordinary books, covered nearly every field: crime, fantasy, historical romance, espionage, Westerns, science fiction, adventure, animal stories, love, war, and fashionable society, big business and big medicine. Eighty motion pictures have been based on his work along with many radio and television programs. For good measure he also published four volumes of poetry. Perhaps no other author has reached more people in more different ways.

Born in Seattle in 1892, orphaned early, Faust grew up in the rural San Joaquin Valley of California. At Berkeley he became a student rebel and one-man literary movement, contributing prodigiously to all campus publications. Denied a degree because of unconventional conduct, he embarked on a series of adventures culminating in New York City where, after a period of near starvation, he received simultaneous recognition as a serious poet and successful popular-prose writer. Later, he traveled widely, making his home in New York, then in Florence, and finally in Los Angeles.

Once the United States entered the Second World War, Faust abandoned his lucrative writing career and his work as a screenwriter to serve as a war correspondent with the infantry in Italy, despite his fifty-one years and a bad heart. He was killed during a night attack on a hilltop village held by the German army. New books based on magazine serials or unpublished manuscripts or restored versions continue to appear so that, alive or dead, he has averaged a new book every four months for seventy-five years. In the United States alone nine publishers now issue his work. Beyond this, some work by him is newly reprinted every week of every year in one or another format somewhere in the world. Yet, only recently have the full dimensions of this extraordinarily versatile and prolific writer come to be recognized and his stature as a protean literary figure in the 20th Century acknowledged. His popularity continues to grow throughout the world.

We hope that you enjoyed reading this
Sagebrush Large Print Western.
If you would like to read more Sagebrush titles,
ask your librarian or contact the Publishers:

United States and Canada

Thomas T. Beeler, *Publisher*
Post Office Box 659
Hampton Falls, New Hampshire 03844-0659
(800) 251-8726

United Kingdom, Eire, and
the Republic of South Africa

Isis Publishing Ltd
7 Centremead
Osney Mead
Oxford OX2 0ES England
(01865) 250333

Australia and New Zealand

Australian Large Print Audio & Video P/L
17 Mohr Street
Tullamarine, Victoria, 3043, Australia
1 800 335 364

LPF BRA   30013001186953
Brand, Max,

Farewell, Thunder Moon